The Pitch

The Pitch

A Clean Romantic Suspense (An Untapped Source Book 4)

Amy Martinsen

This is a work of fiction. Names, characters, organizations, places, events, and incidents are either products of the author's imagination or are used fictitiously. Any resemblance to actual persons, living or dead, or actual events is purely coincidental.

Copyright © 2023 by Amy Martinsen

Cover design by Evelyne Labelle at Carpe Librum Book Design

www.carpelibrumbookdesign.com

All rights reserved. No portion of this book may be reproduced in any form or by any electronic or mechanical means, including information storage and retrieval systems without written permission from the author, except for the use of brief quotations in a book review.

ISBN-979-8-9860635-5-3

Printed in the United States of America

Created with Atticus

Chapter One

I'm not sure whether the sound is human or animal. I stop, close my eyes, and listen. It's an otherwise quiet moment on my street in Kensington—most people have left for work and the school buses have come and gone. I don't need to be at CIA headquarters until noon, so I opted for a quick run through my neighborhood.

The sound comes again. I pull it behind my eyelids and into my mind. It's frantic, filled with pain. From years of honing my tradecraft as a CIA officer, I recognize the vocal flexibility that can only come from a human mouth, tongue, and lips. I open my eyes and scan the neighborhood to pinpoint the source. No luck. It's one of those gray May days that can happen in Maryland, with thick clouds that drop low to the ground, creating a distorted ricochet effect with sound.

"Can you hear me? Where are you?" I shout. If I can hear this person, then, hopefully, they can hear me. My words volley between houses and clouds like a ping-pong ball thrown into a small room.

The sound comes again. This time definitely a scream with the high pitch of an answer—they heard me. It came from the direction I was heading—toward home.

I dart into a full run. The scream repeats every ten steps. It's a female. I try to make out what she's saying. The screams sound as if they come from her gut—wrenching, primal, and desperate.

My heart is pounding in my ears. I stop, forcing the pounding to slow and my breathing to quiet. I'm a block from my home and her voice is still coming from that direction.

"I'm coming. Hang on," I yell to the woman whose body is producing these screams that will own a place in my psyche. The sound has the chunking and cadence of sentences, but I can't match words to it.

Adrenalin slices through my chest as I stop in front of the house across the street from mine—my neighbors for the last four years. The screams are coming from Brittany Hall, the twenty-eight-year-old wife of Guy Hall, an employee at the Pentagon. Brittany is eight months pregnant.

I race to her front door. It's locked but not with a dead bolt. For the second time in as many minutes, adrenalin cuts through me as I register the words Brittany is screaming. She yells to kick in the door. No problem. One swift thrust and I'm in. But what sent a new shock of adrenalin through me is the language these words are in—Russian. And not just any Russian, but a dialect and accent that could only come from someone who lived in the country, possibly even grew up there. How would Brittany Hall, who grew up in Virginia and works as a legal secretary, know Russian like a native?

By the time I make my way through the door to the kitchen where Brittany's lying on the floor, she's screamed enough Russian street swearing to convince me she's spent a good portion of her childhood there. The kitchen windows are open—how I heard her—but the security screens are locked. Somehow Brittany knew kicking the door in would be faster.

I'm dialing 911 as I kneel next to her. The roundness of her child, ready to enter the world, dwarfs her petite form. Brittany's light-brown hair is drenched with sweat and stuck to her cheeks and forehead. Her golden-brown eyes, normally so calm and assured, are crazed with pain. They focus on me, then sag with relief.

"Help is coming. It's going to be okay," I tell her and offer a silent, desperate prayer that it will be.

"Thank you, thank you," Brittany says in Russian.

The 911 operator fires questions to me, most of which I know the answer to. I give the operator Brittany's address and say that she's in labor. There's fluid on her jeans and the floor, so it looks as if her water has broken.

"How many weeks along are you?" I ask Brittany in English.

"Thirty-six. Too early. Too early," she answers me, again in Russian. She doesn't realize she's speaking in what is clearly her native tongue. Another labor pain seizes her, and she moans loudly and begs for her mother. A thought awkwardly niggles at the back of my mind—a sickening, frightening thought I immediately push away.

"Do you need an interpreter?" asks the operator. I assure her we don't. The frightening thought finds its footing and walks to the front of my mind. My tradecraft will not allow me to ignore it.

I hear the sirens in the distance and the operator asks if I want her to stay on the line until the paramedics come.

Knowing emergency services record these calls, I tell the operator no, thank her, and quickly hang up. It's crucial I have a few seconds alone with Brittany. I gently turn her head to direct her eyes toward mine.

"When the paramedics come, you'll need to speak in English," I tell her in Russian. I do my best but I didn't grow up in Russia so my accent and words don't match hers. It's good enough, though. Her eyes lock onto mine and she's silent.

She knows, says the voice in my head, the trusted instinct that has never failed me.

I've heard of officers having moments like this—when the covers are blown and each of you knows who the other is . . . at least a general idea. Brittany knows her neighbor, Kate Ross, doesn't work for the State Department at a job that requires her to travel a lot. And I know Brittany Wilson Hall has been hiding the fact that she's Russian. No words are spoken to confirm this. Words aren't needed. Because of my years of working in the world of espionage—lying, deceiving, hiding—I instantly recognized that Brittany has this same experience. The savage pain of childbirth brought her guard down and I saw behind her cover. And she knows I saw. There's no need to talk about it right now.

Another labor pain grips Brittany, but she remains silent, her teeth grinding as her eyes lock onto mine. The sound of sirens fills the house and, in a few seconds, the paramedics are beside me. They're asking Brittany questions and she's answering them in perfect English. Before they wheel her out, she grabs my arm.

"Call Guy. Tell him where they're taking me," she asks. Her eyes beg me to keep our secret and I nod to both her verbal and nonverbal requests. I'll call her husband and tell him his wife is in labor and what hospital she's going to, but I won't mention anything about her being Russian. I'll make this phone call as I frantically drive to headquarters because I have a hard decision to make and I have to make it now.

Chapter Two

Despite the many aspects of the CIA that Hollywood gets wrong, the one thing they get right is how we dress—dark suits and white shirts. So, when I race across the large CIA emblem on the floor of headquarters and through security in yoga pants and a sweaty T-shirt, it draws some looks. I know I look rough. A glance in the glass door before I entered confirms this—my dark hair is slick with sweat and coming out of its ponytail. With no makeup, the olive skin I inherited from my Iraqi father has nothing to cover the extreme levels of adrenalin my body has absorbed in the past hour, leaving it blotchy and ashen-gray. The red round scar to the side of my left eye looks even more pronounced than usual. My light blue eyes, inherited from my American mother, are dulled by stress on the brink of panic.

I called Brittany's husband, Guy, on the drive here and told him his wife was in labor and what hospital to go to, gulped down the guilt of what I wasn't telling him, and then called headquarters and told them what had happened. The questions of what will become of Guy and this innocent child shoot through my brain like a machine gun. I force them back to be dealt with later. For now, I have to think about Brittany and my next move.

By the time I reach the conference room, everyone is waiting for me. Neal Holt, my boss, stands like the ex-military man he is. He and his wife, Nadine, have been like a second set of parents to me. His blue eyes are riveted on me. I know this look well, having seen it many times in my two operations in the Middle East with Neal as my boss. I've also seen it from Neal, the father figure, when my life was spiraling out of control after losing my agent, Nahla, and the death of my mother. He's patiently controlling the possible hard decisions lining up in his mind. Neal and I have been through a lot together, and I have no problem trusting him with what I'm about to say.

I'm grateful to see my team here. As I move past Neal, my eyes make brief contact with them and they each give me a slight welcoming nod. Not only are these women excellent intelligence officers, but they are also my dear friends.

Denise Reed, a single mom from the Bronx, is tall with short-cropped, dark hair. She wears her CIA dark pants and white blouse like a model, making her dark skin radiant. With a simple pair of gold hoop earrings, she elevates the CIA dress code from boring to glamorous. Denise is standing relaxed, knees slightly bent and weight evenly distributed. Her arms hang effortlessly to her side. Anyone who didn't know her would see her as the picture of calmness—a quality that lends itself to her profiling expertise. But I see her counted breathing—three counts on the inhale, three counts to hold, three to exhale. Denise is working for her calmness.

Eva Calvo stands next to Denise. Eva is a widowed ex–Border Patrol Agent from San Luis, Arizona. Unlike Denise, Eva isn't trying to hide anything. She folds her arms across her chest and rolls back and forth onto the balls of her feet. She's petite and fit, with her long, dark hair pulled back into a ponytail to be out of her way. Eva is ready to get to work—she wants the facts so she can make a plan.

Gina Stoddard sits at the conference table with her laptop in front of her. The clacking of her fingers hitting the keyboard is the only sound in the room. Gina is divorced, from Georgia, and her opinions are as bold as her orange polka-dotted reading glasses balanced on the end of her nose. Though rounder and softer than Denise and Eva, Gina can keep up with any field officer half her age. She's a computer genius and a dead shot with a Glock 19, so no one says anything about her big blonde hair and overdone makeup.

These three older women make up the CIA's secret espionage weapon. They are known as an untapped source—U-Tap—and have earned the respect of everyone at Langley. Who would suspect a middle-aged mom of being a spy? As I look at the three sitting at the conference table, ready to work, pride swells my heart. Gina looks at me over her reading glasses and her enhanced eyebrows come together.

"Hey, honey," Gina says, her fingers never slowing on the keyboard. She only calls me honey when she's really worried about me. Her eyes move back to her computer because I'm sure she's probably two steps ahead of all of us.

The one person I haven't looked at yet stands to my left, just outside my peripheral view. But I know he's here. I felt the pull of him the minute I walked into the room. I turn my body and face John Leeman, and the love for me is there on his face, unmasked for all to see. CIA officers aren't supposed to fall in love with each other, but we did, and it works. Like Gina's nonregulation reading glasses, no one says a thing.

John is tall and handsome, a perfect melding of his Japanese and Caucasian heritage, which gives him a foreign look that could be several different nationalities—an excellent tool for a spy. His exotic eyes hold mine with an unblinking look of concern that would rival Eva's most determined stare.

"Let's sit down," Neal says. Gina is sitting at the end of the conference table, so we sit around her, forming a half circle, everyone facing me. From somewhere, Denise produces a cold can of Coke and sets it in front of me. I gulp down half of it and feel the sugar steady my system. "Start from the beginning," Neal says. "Don't leave anything out."

I start with the first time I hear the sound and go to when I realize Brittany is screaming in Russian.

"Russian?" everyone asks, except Gina. Her hands stop typing and she is staring at me over the top of her laptop.

"Yes, Russian, but not regular Russian. It was a slang, vulgar, street-like Russian, something a native would know," I answer.

"This is Brittany Hall that lives across the street, right? The one you've become friends with?" John asks. I look down at the desk as a wave of sad memories crashes over me.

"Yes, that Brittany," I answer. Mary Hayden was my CIA counselor. During our sessions, she encouraged me to make more friends, to nurture relationships outside of the agency. She felt it would be emotionally healthy for me, even though I thought it was just more people to convince I work for the State Department—my cover.

Mary lost her life protecting me on our last operation, all because I walked into her office as a patient. The guilt sits in my chest like a boulder. Wanting to honor her request, I've been trying to turn the wave-across-the-street relationship I've had with Brittany into more of a friendship.

"Nowhere in our conversations over coffee or a quick lunch did her spending serious time on the streets of Russia come up. John hasn't met Brittany or her husband, Guy, but we were planning to go out to dinner before the baby came. Knowing she's Russian and hiding it, it's probably a good thing she hasn't seen John's face," I say. Knowing looks are exchanged while avoiding my eyes.

"What happened next is why I'm here. Brittany didn't realize she was speaking in Russian and when I told her she'd have to speak in English when the paramedics came, it happened."

"What happened?" Eva asks. Everyone else appeared to be wondering the same thing, but Denise held my eyes with a knowing look.

"In that instant, I knew she was Russian, born and raised there, and I knew she has been hiding it. And she knew I don't work for the State Department. How this happened, I don't know, other than childbirth has a way of taking all the masks off. We saw in each other all the training and hiding and lying we've done," I say. "I've heard of other case officers and agents having moments like this, but I never thought it would happen to me with my neighbor, Brittany."

As I was speaking Gina never stopped typing frantically on her laptop—not an unusual practice of hers because not only is she listening intently, but her mind, through her fingers, is finding answers.

"Y'all, I've heard of this somewhere in history and I just found it," Gina says, pushing her orange polka-dotted readers even further down her nose. "During World War II, the KGB thought they were pulling off the perfect infiltration of female Russian spies into Germany. They trained these women to speak the language flawlessly, know the culture, everything. These Russian ladies were in it for the long game. They were to marry German men who were in some kind of leadership position, have babies, all while stealing what intel they could from their husbands. This is where the Russians messed up big time, because if a woman screams during childbirth, she will almost always scream in her native tongue. The Germans caught a bunch of these Russian sleeper cells in labor and delivery—like that experience needs anymore drama," Gina says with a roll of her eyes.

"But that was World War II, a long time ago. Would Russia still be using this type of tradecraft, especially when it failed so spectacularly?" John asks.

"Wasn't there a case around the turn of the century where illegals from Russia were living in the US as Americans so they wouldn't have the scrutiny that other diplomatically protected spies would have?" Denise asks.

"Yes," Neal answers. "They trained these Russian illegals from a young age to be Americans. English was their first language. They probably knew more about American culture and history than most of us. Putin was climbing up the ranks of power in Russia and we believe he was behind this operation. We watched these sleeper cells for ten years before we got them."

"Ten years?" Eva asks.

"Yep. Because we never found a purpose for their spying. We never found out why Russia and Putin would go to such an enormous cost and effort to train a group of sleeper cells and plant them here, then not have them do anything. Was it an ego trip on Putin's part, to show Russia he could beat us at counterintelligence in our own backyard?" Neal asks. We sit in silence for a few seconds, absorbing the enormity of this information. Gina even stops typing.

"But this is Russia we're talking about," Gina says. "They don't play by the rules. Neither do a lot of countries. But where China's spying is cold, impersonal, self-serving, Russian spying is driven by Putin's personal hatred for the US. He wants to regain the power of the old Soviet Union and will do anything to get it. Spying without a purpose is immoral, but Putin doesn't give a rat's patootie about that."

"What if there's just some part of Brittany's past that she hasn't shared with you?" Eva asks. "Was she a foreign exchange student? Did she travel to Russia with a tour group? Could she have Russian relatives she could have picked up some of this language from?" Eva's interrogation skills are kicking in and I appreciate her questions because I know the answers and they solidify what the voice in my head told me—that Brittany and I know things about each other that we've been hiding. I'm CIA and she's SVR—the

Russian Foreign Intelligence Service formerly known as the KGB, Russia's answer to the CIA. I shake my head.

"Brittany has told me about her schooling and she wouldn't have left out something as big as spending time studying in Russia. And she's always talking about how amazed she is with Guy's ability to speak several languages, none of which are Russian."

We sit in silence for a few more seconds as the pressure of the decision we need to make looms closer.

"What does your gut tell you?" Neal asks. I stare at him for a few seconds, trying to order my thoughts, and then give up. Every minute that goes by is a minute I need to plan.

"My gut tells me that Brittany's SVR, and she's terrified that her cover is blown by someone in the CIA—the worst possible scenario for a Russian spy. I think she's going to go for the pitch. She's going to try to turn me to save her cover. It's an enormous risk but I saw in her eyes she's desperate enough to try. Whatever she's involved in must have a purpose, a big purpose. I don't think Putin's just playing around this time," I say.

"From what you've told us, I'd have to agree," Denise says. "To say this girl is in deep is a massive understatement. She would try anything to save her cover. And it would be quite the win for her to offer up a CIA officer to Mother Russia."

"Do I have what it takes to be a double agent?" I whisper, more to myself than the others. I notice Gina's eyebrows coming together in confusion, so I continue. "To Russia, I'll be a recruited agent, but to American intelligence, I'm a double agent. Being a double agent is another level of spying altogether and why those who do it are considered to be in an espionage class of their own. It's one thing to be a case officer, running foreign assets in the field—keeping them safe, running surveillance, managing dead drops, and sending intel up the line. It's a whole different ball game to sit across from a Russian spy and convince them you hate your country enough to offer its precious secrets on a silver platter, all the while remaining loyal to your country."

"So, wait. Y'all are confusing me," Gina says "Now you're an agent?" Gina came to the agency like so many people, with an engrained belief that anyone who works for the CIA is called an agent. Much to her dismay, she learned that those employed by the CIA are referred to as officers. The foreign people we recruit to spy on their countries for us are called agents. It is the same for British intelligence. The new use of these terms was especially hard for Gina, being a rabid James Bond fan, which is why our team refers to agents as assets.

"To clarify, you can't be a double agent without having first been an agent. When Kate accepts Brittany's pitch, Kate will become a Russian agent for the SVR. But because Kate remains loyal to American intelligence, she will then be a double agent," Neal says.

"Okay, well, at least that isn't complicated," Gina responds with sarcasm. "I should probably quit watching James Bond movies, but that ain't ever gonna happen." This garners a few chuckles, but I'm too anxious to do more. I clench and unclench my fists because the clock keeps ticking. I need to get us back on topic.

"Look, every minute that goes by that the FBI doesn't show up at the hospital to question Brittany adds confidence to her pitch. She knows I'm thinking about it," I say. "Either that, or she's planning how to run. I don't think she'll run, though."

"Why don't you give it a few hours and then reach out to Guy? It would be normal for you to follow up and see how she is," Neal says. "If she's desperate to save whatever her mission is, this will give her time to plan a good pitch and also prove to her your willingness to hear it. It will also give us some time to think and plan." I nod, then look over at John. His face is a combination of concern and encouragement, and I know what he's thinking.

"She's probably not working alone. If there are other spies like Brittany out there, we have a chance of finding them, of stopping whatever they have planned. We all know just what kind of damage a group of sleeper cells can do," I say to John. He and I exchange a nonverbal understanding about his ex-wife, Clare, the mother of his daughter, Olivia. Clare's in the ADX Florence Supermax prison in Colorado, the result of our team learning she was a radicalized terrorist. This isn't our first rodeo with sleeper cells. But this is Russia and despite their lack of childbirth knowledge, they still are considered the best when it comes to the long game . . . and the best in the world at detecting liars. Which brings me back to the question that has been creeping up from my stomach—can I outsmart the Russians at lying?

Chapter Three

John walks me back through the entrance so I can go home, shower, and dress to look like a CIA officer for a planning meeting in two hours. We walk slowly, quietly across the black-and-gray emblem I ran across a little while ago. I can't help but glance at the stars on the wall—The CIA Memorial Wall—honoring those who gave their lives to find out information. I've felt the brush of that wall a few times, but nothing like the fear that thrums in my heart right now. Already I feel separate, removed from this place. Unprotected.

As soon as John and I walk through the glass doors, he takes my hand. His touch is warm and familiar, and it pulls me back to who I am. My other hand instinctively reaches up and touches the gold circle that hangs from a delicate chain around my neck. The necklace was John's Christmas gift to me, symbolizing that I'm a part of his circle that includes his mother, Rose, and daughter, Livvy. These are my people and their relationships are real.

We remain silent until we reach my black Tahoe in the parking lot. The gray clouds outline the vehicle's blackness. Everything is black and gray today.

"You don't have to do this if you don't want to," John says.

You must do this, says the voice in my head. I nod to both because they're both right.

"I know, and I'm grateful you said that. But I have to do this." I hold his dark eyes, the only blackness that makes me feel safe in this day. "John, I saw her. *Really* saw her. Who she is. I knew in that instant that she's spent her life training to find out our secrets." John keeps my gaze and then slowly grins.

"You have your father's instinct," he says. My father, the MI6 legend I thought had abandoned me as a child, but who really went into hiding to protect my mother and me. He's the reason I'm still alive, with only a small scar next to my left eye to show for the chemical weapon he saved me from. I'm no James McLean, my father's MI6 name, or Ammar Rasheed, his name from birth. But I guess John would be a better judge of that, having worked with my father undercover before he ever knew me.

"Okay, say I *can* pull off being a double agent. What will it do to me?" I ask. A shadow crosses his eyes. He's done this sort of spying before, though he hasn't told me much about it.

"We'll help you. I'll help you. You'll be able to keep it all straight."

"By 'it' do you mean my soul? Because that's what I'm talking about," I say. I watch his eyes closely. They hint of something, perhaps memories, he's trying to forget. He pulls me to him and the clean smell of his cologne sooths and slows my heart.

"Go home and get something to eat. You'll feel better. And then we'll make a plan together. You won't be alone.

I'll be with you the whole way." I nod against his white dress shirt and stay in his hug as long as I need to.

A shower and food help. Sometimes it's something as simple as clean hair and a turkey sandwich that will bring some normalcy back for a few moments. The sight of Brittany and Guy's house across the street, though, and what just happened there, makes it all feel as different as if someone had erected a neon sign in their front yard: Russian spy lives here.

I call Guy's phone on my drive back to headquarters, but the call goes to voice mail. No news is good news at this point, and I offer a prayer for Brittany and her baby and the future of that child. This concern leads to my continual prayer for John's sweet daughter, Livvy, who will eventually learn who her mother is and I pray every day that the Lord will strengthen Livvy to handle that knowledge. I have to keep pushing these thoughts back for later or they will cloud my judgment.

Dressed in a black skirt and white blouse, my damp hair twisted into a bun on top of my head, I try to walk calmly through the entrance of headquarters and back across the black-and-gray emblem. I look like any other officer showing up for work. But my mouth is dry and my hands have a slight tremor as I hand my purse through security. I'm sure my blood pressure is anything but normal, and sweat beads cluster on my top lip. These are all signs of distress that I'll need to keep in check to be a double agent—there will always be people watching me . . . and I'll have to let them watch me.

Neal, John, and the team are waiting for me in the conference room. Everyone has a Starbucks cup in their hand and one waits for me on the table. Gina bought mine because it has whipped cream and sprinkles on top. I give her a smile of thanks and take my first sip. The sweet, caffeine-rich coffee reaches all the way to my toes.

We sit in the same seats as before—so everyone can see me—except for John, who pulls his chair close to mine and rests his arm on the back of my chair. He doesn't need to see my face to know what I'm feeling. Relief sinks me deep into my chair and I lean back, feeling the brush of John's hand. My spy brain has been trying to put together a plan, but I've only been able to produce a few panic-driven thoughts. Most officers have months to prepare for this level of espionage work. I'll probably have a few hours.

"I tried calling Guy on the way back here, but it went to voice mail. I'll wait for him to call me back," I say to get the meeting started. Everyone nods.

"It's good to not look too anxious," Denise says. There are a few seconds of silence that follow. I lean forward and pick up my pen but have nothing to write. As reassuring as this group is, I feel the clock ticking. I need a plan.

"So, what do I do when she pitches me?" I ask. It's not "if" but "when." I don't want to waste time discussing the chance that she won't. I know she will.

"Let's look at the timeline first," Eva says. "How soon do you think she'll make the pitch?"

"I think she'll do it soon. There was clear desperation in her eyes and it wasn't just from pain," I say.

"Her cover is blown—a cover she's spent her life to create. She'll probably ignore all the normal vetting protocols and take the first opportunity to approach you," Denise says.

"She'll most likely give birth in the next few hours," Gina says. "Most insurance companies will cover a hospital stay between twenty-four to forty-eight hours after birth for a normal delivery. That would put her coming home tomorrow evening at the very earliest." Gina types on her laptop, and I exhale. A plan is happening.

"We won't know for sure until we hear from Guy. He'll call. An excited new father will be eager to share the news with the person who helped his wife," Eva says. We all give a quick nod, and I mentally set the timeline aside in my mind. Maybe I'll have more time to prepare than I think.

"I've made a list of a few things that will make this operation unique and easier for you," Neal says. I give Neal a smile, the first for today.

"'Easier' is the word I need to hear," I say. This gets a little chuckle from the group.

"Of course, you'll be meeting with Audrey after you've been pitched. But there's no reason we can't start prepping right away," Neal says. Audrey Brier took over counterintelligence after Norman Steele's abrupt and questionable departure at the end of our last operation. Steele is an arrogant man obsessed with staying young. If he has one more plastic surgery, no one will recognize him.

From what I hear, Officer Brier is making a smooth transition despite the chaos and is highly respected by the agency. The thought of trying to maneuver a double agent operation with Norman Steele makes me ill. Anyone would be better. But I don't know Officer Brier or what she'll be like to work with. I'm not trying to hide anything and the concern shows on my face.

"Audrey is a good person. You can trust her," Neal adds.

"Thanks," I say. If Neal thinks she can be trusted, then she can.

"One of our biggest advantages is that Brittany and her people will believe you are an in-place penetration. They'll think you'll always be worrying about protecting your position with the CIA. You, of course, won't have that, but you'll have to convince Brittany that you are, indeed, looking over your shoulder," Neal says. He's right.

"If I was a defector seeking asylum here in America, I would be considered a much safer risk. As a defector, I would have left my life behind, so there would be no one to catch me giving away my country's secrets," I say.

"So, to Miss Brittany, you're the highest risk possible, sitting smack-dab in the middle of a bunch of spy catchers. It's another sign of just how desperate she may be to consider pitching you," Gina says.

"Brittany knows that you have years of training and experience, but she doesn't know just how good you are. The fact that you're one of the best street spies I've known, especially with surveillance, will be another advantage for you," Neal says. I give him a grin of thanks, but the familiar guilt twists my stomach. Having lost an agent in the field—Nahla, an outstanding agent and dear friend who I was supposed to protect—I don't know if I'll ever be able to be comfortable with a compliment like this.

THE PITCH

"I'll need to brush up on a few things," I say. It's been a while since I've had people following me on the street, and I'm sure with the Russians, it will be a small army tailing me.

"That's what we're here for," Denise says and reaches over to pat my hand. She spent years on the streets in New York, disguised, studying street gangs. She and the ladies will provide me the Russian-level of surveillance strategies I'll need.

"And last, but certainly not least, you'll have the constant emotional support of this group and the backing of the agency behind you," Neal says.

"That's huge," I say, the words catching in my throat. Most double agents do their work completely alone, making dead drops of intel to unknown connections, never knowing if the intel they've risked their life for will ever make a difference or even get to the right people. There's no one to talk to about their complex lives, no sounding boards.

"Y'all will have everything you need. Don't you worry," Gina says over her typing.

"These are some strong advantages. It will probably be more work hiding them than we think. But what am I going to use to convince Brittany that I hate this country? That I'm willing to give up secrets and turn into a traitor?" I ask. I really only have one idea, but will it hold water?

"Your father," John says, quietly.

Chapter Four

My father left my mother and me when I was just a few months old. My mother never talked about him, so my young mind filled in the blanks with the worst it could conjure up. Until last year, I hated my father, hanging onto the false beliefs that were entrenched in my heart.

And then by chance—or a tender mercy from God—I met my father and learned the truth. He's a spy who had to leave the ones he loved to protect them, and he's been hiding ever since. Although, according to my father, he knows the people who are after him—the people who cost him a lifetime without his daughter and the wife he dearly loved. He claims he knows these people better than anyone else and knows how to avoid them. I don't doubt him. His careful attention to detail, along with his incredible spy instinct, has made him a legend in the world of espionage. But he's still running, still constantly looking over his shoulder, and trusting very few people. That's no way to live.

I've secretly vowed to myself to find these people and put an end to my father's running, despite his explicit warning not to. If I have inherited his instinct, then one day I can put it to good use and help him. For now, though, I need to use him as an excuse to turn into a traitor. The father I've come to know will understand. I look at Neal and then at John. They know this world better than anyone at this table.

"Is it enough? A girl denied a relationship with her father because he was a spy. Will Brittany and Mother Russia buy this?" I ask.

"It will be enough because you'll be able to sell it. Even though you don't hate him now, you spent many years feeling that emotion for your father. You know what it's like. You can tap into that hate," Neal says.

"But I know now why my father did what he did to protect us. That's pretty powerful. Will I be able to keep that from showing?" I ask.

"You compartmentalize it, just like any other cover," Neal says. I nod, knowing well this mental and emotional strategy, though I've never had to apply it in a situation like this. Usually, I'm the handler teaching a foreign asset how to manage their emotions while deceiving others. I look over at John, but he is noticeably quiet. I know there are large gaps in his career that he can't talk about to anyone, but I could really use some advice now.

"It's important to remember," Denise says as I pull my eyes from John to her, "that the idea of you holding a grudge about your father's absence will hold more weight with Russia than you think. They view Americans as weak, especially regarding our need for human connection and relationships. Emotions are a weakness to Soviet ideology. So, would an American sell out her country for having been emotionally wronged? They think so. And they're more than happy to exploit what they consider our emotional neediness."

"That makes sense," I say. "I've never spoken to Brittany about my parents. She's asked, but I've changed the subject. I've tried to form a friendship with her, like I was encouraged by . . ." I pause for a second, not wanting to say Mary's name. It's still too soon for me. "It just felt like there were too many things to sidestep. But this could work for me. The topic of my father can appear as something I've buried—too painful to talk about. More the reason to seek revenge."

"Right. Spend tonight working through that. Get your mind back in that place of anger," Neal says. I nod to Neal and then glance over at John, but he remains silent.

"I can send you some profiling information focusing on anger. There's a site I like that has some great information on revenge," Denise says.

"I know which one you're talking about," Gina says as she types. "I'm sending it now."

"That will be helpful," I say. The table falls silent. Just when I'm about to ask John if he has anything to add, he speaks.

"This won't change you, being a double agent. The Lord won't let it, not if you're doing it for the right reason, which you are." John's words strike at the core of my fear.

"How can you be certain of that?" I ask. He's silent for a few seconds, but I see on his face that he's collecting his thoughts.

"All the time I was undercover, I clung to a scripture that kept me sane. It's in Isaiah 26. It says that the Lord will keep in perfect peace those whose minds are steadfast, because they trust Him. If we trust the Lord, He will be a source of everlasting strength for us," John says. The words melt into my chest and calm me. Can my mind really stay in perfect peace while pretending to be a traitor to my country? My eyes burn with tears of relief at the thought.

"I've never read that scripture," I say, throaty with emotion.

"I hadn't either until your father read it to me. James McLean saved me many times in the field, but never more than when he read me this scripture. I was tanking emotionally, but those words helped me get my head right, to keep in focus the 'why' of what I was doing, and that I was worthy of help from the Lord," John says.

Tears break free and roll down my cheeks. Could I be worthy of this same help? I wipe the tears away as more come. I'm not afraid to cry in front of these people. John hands me his ever-present cloth handkerchief and I put it to good use. He always has one with him.

"I guess my father's saving me again," I say.

"That's what good fathers do. They save their daughters," Neal says. I smile and nod through tears. My phone rings and I jump at the loud, intrusive sound at such a tender moment. It's Guy. I wipe my face and exhale through one more ring, then answer.

"Do we have a baby?" I ask, nothing but excited congratulations in my voice.

"We do! We have a beautiful, healthy girl," Guy says. He's speaking loudly and everyone at the table can hear him through my phone.

"How's Brittany? Is she okay?" I ask.

"She's doing great. We just can't thank you enough. I mean, I don't know what would have happened if you hadn't come running by when you did," he says.

"Well, we won't think about that. All that matters is that Brittany and your daughter are okay. And you're a dad now," I say.

"I am," he says through laughter. "We'll be home tomorrow evening. Brittany wants to get out of here as soon as she can. We'd love for you to come over." He pauses for a minute and I hear what sounds like Brittany's voice in the background. "Brittany says you have to come over as soon as we get home. She wants to thank you personally." At this request, I scan the eyes around the table. That Brittany wants to see me as soon as possible and not just to thank me bounces between us.

"Of course. I'll watch for you," I say. He thanks me again and we end the call.

"She'll pitch you tomorrow," Denise says.

She's right, says the voice in my head. *You'll be ready.*

"We'll all be there, watching with you," John says. "I'll be safe. I doubt she'll have the house watched just yet. If it were me, I wouldn't tell my people my cover's been compromised until I had a plan to save the operation, like a turned CIA officer."

"I'll make something for you to take over for their dinner," Eva says.

"And I'll stop by the mall on the way home and pick up a gift for y'all to take," Gina adds.

"I'll go with you," Denise says to Gina. "There are a few things I need."

"We'll take care of everything else. Just focus on selling your revenge," Eva says. I smile at these women who I love and respect so much. They have my back.

"I will. Thank you," I say.

"They should be done sweeping your house for bugs," Neal says, signaling the end of the meeting. It's time for me to go home and prepare. I exhale and stand. I have a long, hard night ahead of me.

Chapter Five

My house has more signs of life than it ever has—it looks like a person with relationships lives here. A white milk glass vase holds a large bunch of pink hydrangeas, their full blooming heads crowding each other for space. The vase is on "loan" from John's mother, Rose, and the hydrangeas are from her garden. John picked these particular flowers, knowing how much I love them.

A stack of coloring books, crayons and markers, and several dolls take up a third of my sofa—all things I've collected and keep out for whenever Livvy visits with John. Below them on the floor is a pair of purple glittery clogs that Livvy left here a few days ago, the weather being warm enough that she played barefoot in my backyard and forgot all about shoes when she left.

These signs of life always make me happy to be home, but nothing pulls me in like what covers my fridge—all the pictures Livvy draws for me. I grab a pint of rocky road ice cream—my dinner of choice after a hard day—and sit on the kitchen counter so I can be eye level with the drawings. Each paper has at its center Livvy's interpretation of me. She used to fill up the rest of the space with stars but has moved on to flowers, suns, and clouds—all images she's learned to draw in preschool.

I spoon ice cream into my mouth and let my gaze move from one face to the next. When I first met Livvy, she called me Kate with the pretty eyes. Each image of me has light-blue eyes with long, dark hair. My mouth, though, is different in each drawing. One looks cartoon-happy with a silly open-mouthed grin and the next almost sad in comparison. Children sense emotions better than anyone, even a trained spy. Is this what Livvy has done in these drawings? Unaware of the feelings I was showing to those around me, did Livvy record them with a simple paper and crayon? I wasn't trying to hide anything in the moments Livvy drew these—I was free and safe to share my feelings. Now, though, a large part of my life will be calculated, even down to the slightest nuance.

I put my half-eaten pint of ice cream back in the freezer and sit back on the counter. I should get my laptop out and read the profiling articles Denise and Gina sent me, but I don't want to leave this space of emotional safety that Livvy has created. It holds me like the hug from someone who loves me no matter what face I'm showing. Will I be able to come back to this space when this operation is over? *Remember the scriptures*, says the voice in my head. *Let them be your foundation.*

I lean over and pick up my bible from the end of the counter and turn to Isaiah 26, to the scriptures John paraphrased in our meeting.

3. Thou wilt keep him in perfect peace whose mind is stayed on thee:
because he trusteth in thee.
4. Trust ye in the Lord forever: for in the Lord JEHOVAH is everlasting strength.

The verses steady me as if stepping from a tossing boat onto solid ground. They are a foundation I can trust. I bring my bible with me to the table and open my laptop.

The articles on anger are a thorough review of how a spy can channel this powerful emotion for the field. I close my eyes and take a deep, cleansing breath, from the bottom of my belly to the top of my head the way Denise has taught me. I reach back into my memories and pull forward the hurt and anger that accompanied every childhood thought of my father. There were always so many unanswered questions. Why did he leave us? Where is he? What is he like? And the biggest question of all was why my mother answered none of these questions.

The frustration of the unknown would often bring tears that I would hold back and then shed alone in my room. I didn't want anyone, especially my mother, to know how much my father's absence hurt me. I try to bring up this frustration, but its once cutting sharpness is dulled by the truth—my father was and is a good man who made the excruciating decision to leave his family in order to protect them. And nobody, including my mother, knew where he was. Right now, I have no idea where he is. I try to push away these truths, but it's like pretending I don't know the end of the story when I do. The "how does it end" holds no water. In my line of work, the truth is what we spend weeks, months, even years seeking. Once we know the truth, it changes everything.

I take a few more deep breaths and remember the day I overheard our neighbor call my father a terrorist. I didn't know what the word meant, but after I looked it up in the dictionary, I was devastated. From that day on, I asked no more questions because I didn't want to know anything about my father. I try to go back to that moment when I felt a part of my heart shut off, but the relief finds a way in—the relief that not only is my father not a terrorist, but also that he has risked his life many times to find and bring to justice some of the worst terrorists in the world. This kind of relief won't be denied, no matter how hard I try. Panic creeps in. How am I going to convince Brittany of traitor-level anger . . . tomorrow?

I close my eyes again and offer a prayer for help, and then I breathe and listen. The words of the scriptures move across my mind's eye, and I imagine a firm foundation—a stone floor, sure and solid, under my bare feet. The weight of my body can evenly balance on the cool, stable surface. I take a step forward; my toes instinctively grip to balance against any movement but then relax against the unyielding rock. Nothing is moving beneath me. Everything is as it seems. I take another step and then another, trusting my feet on the stone underneath them. My legs move with ease, each footfall followed by another. I'm moving forward with sure strength. I can get to where I need to be.

What if Livvy lost her father like you lost yours? asks the voice in my head.

My eyes fly open as adrenalin burns up my arms and neck. My throat tightens and I gasp to keep it open. My breathing hasn't been the same since my encounter with a chemical weapon—the one my father saved me from. I race to the kitchen and sip some cold water. Slow, controlled breathing through my nose convinces my mind that air is readily available, that there's no need for panic.

Like Denise has taught me, the breath controls the mind, and the body follows the mind. The adrenalin is lessening in my system, but the question remains.

What *if* Livvy has to pay the same price I have—a life without her father? I look at the glass of water and want to throw it against the wall. I want to scream. I want to hurt someone. I take another sip of water and a long, controlled breath through pursed lips. Anger coils in the pit of my stomach, controlled for now, but looking for a reason to strike.

With the glass of water close by, I sit at my laptop and start typing. My mind clicks into motion, fleshing out several scenarios with Brittany and my responses to each. I now have an authentic source of anger, one that will convince even the most skeptical Russian agent that I mean business in selling out my country.

Chapter Six

FBI Special Agent Rolland Maxwell eases his solid girth against my kitchen counter as he downs a large frosted donut in three bites. Sprinkles cling to the taut fabric of his white shirt like climbers who have lost their anchor. Maxwell doesn't notice and wouldn't care if he did. I don't care, either. Optional grooming is a small part of who Maxwell is. I've discovered there's much more to the man once you get past his brusque demeanor and unappealing habits. He's an excellent agent, loyal friend and husband, and will do anything to protect me. This last quality I discovered two operations ago when I learned my father had somehow saved Maxwell years ago on an operation that went south. I know nothing else except that Maxwell feels he owes my father, and the only way to pay him back is to protect me.

Someday, I hope to know more about this relationship between my father and Maxwell. It would be another piece of the puzzle that is my father's past. But for now, I have a gruff but committed FBI special agent who has my back. By sundown, I'll either have declared myself a traitor to the Russians or need Maxwell to arrest my neighbor. Either way, it's good to have Maxwell here this morning. I made an early donut run, knowing he was coming.

John was here when I got back from getting donuts—an hour before everyone else was to show up. It was an hour of quiet alone time together, something we rarely have. With clear May sunshine coming through my front window, I told him of the experience I had the night before and the inspired answer to my prayer. John kissed me like he does when we're alone and then promised me Livvy would always have her father and he would always be here for me. It's a promise we both know he can't make, especially in our line of work. But that he wants to make this promise so badly that he'll say the words means everything to me.

The sun is further along its daily rotation, casting indirect light through my front window where John stands waiting and watching the Halls' house. It's hours before they'll come home, but John acts as if they could pull in any minute. He stands ready, assuming nothing—one of the basic rules of espionage. John also watches so I don't have to, so I can be inside my mind in the world of hypotheticals. I reviewed with John all the pitch scenarios I came up with last night. He added a few more to my list and practiced with me how I would respond. Now I need to be quiet.

I know I can bring up convincing anger. I just can't let Brittany see past it—I can't let her see the truth. My emotions must convey a genuine energy, and no one knows this better than a well-trained Russian spy. Something tells me Brittany is one of the best. If it were going to be just Brittany and me, this encounter would be easier. But I'll be there with Guy and their daughter—both of whom will have their lives permanently changed no matter how this situation turns out. The thought curdles the coffee in my stomach and I set my cup in the sink.

At noon, Denise, Gina, and Eva come, carrying gift bags exploding with pink tissue paper and a casserole in a disposable pan. There's more talk and more questions. I quickly explain my strategy to channel anger, wanting to withdraw back inside myself. I feel like an actor preparing for a performance. But no actor I know has the pressure of a group of Russian sleeper cells going underground because of a poor performance.

I watch Denise speak quietly to Gina and Eva, and then all three go into the kitchen, leaving me with John in the front room. Denise has had plenty of "performances" before she came to the agency, so she must understand my need for solitude. There's no pressure to speak to John. We are comfortably silent together.

At one o'clock, Eva hands me a plate with a sandwich on it. I get down a few bites and then hand the rest to John, who finishes it. I watch the window more carefully. If they're coming home when Guy said, they could be here anytime.

At two o'clock, I leave John staring out the window while I make a quick trip to the bathroom. When I come back into the front room, John's no longer looking at the Halls' home, but at me.

"They're here," he says.

Chapter Seven

The microphone is a round, flat piece of metal that is glued to the back of my earring. It's an eighth of an inch in diameter and is the same gun metal as my earrings. The microphone will pick up everything Brittany and I say so headquarters can record it. We will analyze every nuance of sound for days, trying to extract all the intended meanings and a thorough profile on Brittany.

Brittany has seen these earrings several times before. They're nothing new, along with the jeans, knit T-shirt, and sandals—all clothes Brittany has seen before. I'll have nothing in my pockets and no other jewelry on. She'll be looking for something new and out of the ordinary. She'll be looking at everything because if she's as well-trained as I believe she is, she'll be worried that I'm doing exactly what I'm doing—trying to trick her so I can find out what she's up to and who she's working with. The clothes I'm wearing are not only familiar but also show I'm not concealing anything like a bulky recording device the CIA hasn't used in years, a phone, or a weapon.

The team and I have planned to wait a half hour after the Halls arrive home before I go over. We use this time to give the microphone a last test and coordinate with headquarters to make sure they're set to record. Neal will be listening in there as well as everyone here at my house. At first, I was worried about "wearing a wire" as we still call it, wondering if it would make it harder to keep my cover convincing with everyone listening. But now, just moments away from my "performance," it's a much-needed connection to what's real.

"Remember, she'll be watching your breathing," Denise says. Denise is right. A change in breathing patterns—shallow and out of breath breathing—is a dead giveaway of a lying person. Denise is worried because my breathing has been so hard to control since the incident with the chemical weapon. I only told John about my struggle last night and now the memory drops like a stone in my stomach.

I can sit across from an asset and know what's in their mind, know what they're feeling, know when they're going to blink, and know by the way they breathe what their next move will be. It only takes a few moments for me to know if they're truthful or lying. But now I'm the asset being analyzed.

Can I do this?

Eva and Gina load my arms up with the gift bags containing two pink outfits, a white blanket, and toys I haven't seen yet, as well as the container with the casserole. Maxwell maneuvers his way in front of me, his large face sweating, though it's cool inside my house. His shirt, still dotted with the clinging sprinkles, is unbuttoned at the collar, allowing his bulging neck to sag freely. His eyes hold mine with an unblinking focus that he must have picked up from Eva.

THE PITCH

"If I hear even the slightest hint of danger, I'm coming in, code word or not," Maxwell says. "And I can have the house surrounded in less than a minute. My team is just waiting for the go-ahead from me." The vein on Maxwell's forehead is pulsing so quickly it's hard to count—a micro expression that he's clearly not trying to control now. I give him a smile, grateful for his over-protection, but I don't want him jumping the gun. He's nervous and has told me all this several times this morning. He doesn't return the smile, but rarely does Rolland Maxwell smile.

"You *will* wait for the code word because I'll be fine. Brittany wants to pitch me, I know it," I say, trying to assure him. We've decided that if I feel threatened at all, I'm to use the word *grapes*. It's a word I can easily work into a conversation without tipping off Brittany, but not such a common word that I would accidentally say it and blow the whole thing.

"You may think she's vulnerable enough, having just had a kid, that she won't try anything. But she's Russian intelligence, and she's married a man she doesn't give a flying you-know-what about and had his kid so she can perform her mission. She's capable of *anything*. You remember that," he says. Maxwell is right on every count. But Brittany's also desperate to save her deep cover, so the riskiest thing she'll do in the next few hours is ask me to join her mission. I don't remind Maxwell of this, though. I need to stay focused and making my point will only be a distraction. I smile again and nod. He's neither convinced nor satisfied. No true protector is until the threat of danger is gone.

During this exchange with Maxwell, John has been watching the Halls' home with an occasional look to me, but now his eyes are fully on mine.

"You should go," John says. "You've prepared enough. Now let it all step back and focus on your instinct."

He's right. Listen to me. I'll be with you every step of the way, says the voice in my head.

"I will," I answer, but my voice cracks and I sound frightened. Probably because I am.

"Chuck every plan, every scenario you've practiced if it doesn't feel right," John continues. "And remember, there's no set way to do this. There's just what this situation requires. Don't compare yourself to me or Neal or your father." I exhale and then thank him because these comparisons were exactly what was going through my mind right now.

Since my hands are full, John opens the front door for me. I offer my team and him the most confident smile I can, but it probably looks more like a painful wince. I take a deep inhale of cool May air and step across the threshold.

Chapter Eight

The storm that came through last night lowered the temperature and dropped the humidity. The sky is a cloudless periwinkle blue, and the air smells of mossy grass from the lawns in the neighborhood. All these elements combine to help me do what I need to do between my doorstep and Brittany's.

Our emotions carry powerful energy others can feel. Despite how masterfully a person can hide what they're feeling by changing their voice, facial expressions, and body language, the energy of their emotions can easily give them away to a well-trained spy. Much of my training in espionage has been to be in tune with the energy around me. I assume Brittany has received this training as well. That's why with each step I take toward her door, I'm orienting my emotions from dread and fear to one of the most powerful emotions there is—hope.

I know things about Brittany, things she's been hiding, and she knows I know them. She also knows I have a pretty good idea why she's hiding it all—to get classified information from her husband, who works at the Pentagon, and give it to whomever her handler is. This is her motive. Brittany knows I work in intelligence and knows why I keep it a secret—why I tell most people in my life that I work for the State Department. Brittany knows what my job is, but she doesn't know my motive. In her vulnerable state of childbirth, I could see a glimpse of her heart, but she hadn't seen into mine. So, from the very first moment of this visit, I'll be fueling my emotions with hope.

Most often, the word *hope* conjures up good intentions—well-intended, worthwhile pursuits. But hope can also be for revenge, to get even, to make someone or something pay a price. I pray this is the hope vibe rolling off of me.

The Halls' house is a two-story colonial and is one of the nicer, larger homes on the street. There's a cement walk that divides their lawn in half and leads directly to the front door. Red tulips line each side of the walk, and tall ivy-covered topiaries flank the front door. Someone has roughly fixed the lock on the door where I kicked it in. I step onto a brown bristly mat with the word *welcome* on it in black script, and ring the doorbell. Two chimes sound and I exhale the last of my nerves as quick, thudding footsteps come closer. The door swings open and Guy Hall fills the space.

"Kate, I'm so glad to see you. And you didn't need to bring all this," he says, motioning to the gifts and food I'm holding. Guy is just a few inches taller than I am and has the stocky, solid build of a football player. He played some in college but went into the Navy and now works in that department at the Pentagon. This is all I know about his work, but I bet Brittany knows more, much more. I squash a sick feeling before the emotion registers.

"I'm so happy for you," I say, "and I'm so glad Brittany and the baby are doing well." Guy's boyish face beams with a smile that fills his brown eyes. His thick reddish-brown hair looks like it spent the night on a sofa and his clothes are crumpled—not the normal Navy-pressed he usually wears. But he's oblivious to his looks right now. He's both exhausted and exhilarated, like I'm sure most first-time fathers are.

"Come in, come in," he says and steps aside for me to enter. He takes the casserole from my right hand and he motions for me to follow him into the kitchen.

"Can I pay for that broken lock? I *am* the one who broke it," I say.

"Absolutely not. I'm so glad you kicked the door in," he says and sets the casserole on the kitchen counter. I set the gift bags next to it. My eyes move to the spot on the floor where I found Brittany yesterday. "I have the locksmith coming later this afternoon. That's some kick you've got there."

"Adrenalin. It's an amazing drug," I say with a smile.

"You got that right," Brittany says from behind me. "It's got me out of some tight spots." I didn't hear or feel her come up behind me. I turn and my eyes lock on hers, and for a split second I catch the real meaning of what she said. Guy laughs at his wife's comment, missing our nonverbal exchange. Guy's imagined tight spots his wife is alluding to isn't anything like what she really means and clearly intended for me alone to understand.

I smile my hopeful, happy smile and embrace Brittany. She's pulled her brown hair back into a ponytail and is wearing yoga pants and a loose-fitting tunic that hides her midsection. Her petite form, though, looks much like before she became pregnant.

Brittany holds my hug a few seconds longer. Is it to truly thank me for helping her, or is it to create a deeper bond that will serve her purpose later?

When I pull away, I ignore the pleading look in her eyes and give her a hefty dose of hope. It confuses her for a second, but that's all the time she takes to switch gears and get what's coming at her. Maybe she'll feel confident to move more quickly toward the pitch.

"Have you told her yet?" Guy asks Brittany. Without breaking eye contact with me, Brittany smiles and shakes her head.

"We're going to name her Kate, after you," she says.

Oh, Brittany's good. She's really good. I didn't see this coming. I look from Brittany's face with its "gotcha" expression to Guy's with his look of loving honor and gratitude, and it's as if I'm between two very different worlds.

"Well, I don't know what to say. I'm so honored. I can't wait to see her," I say, all the right emotions rolling off of me, all laced with hope.

"She's napping in her bassinet in the baby's room. We'll go back and take a peek in a minute," Brittany says. "Guy, why don't you run to the store and get that stuff I need so Kate and I can have some time to chat." She wants to get him out of the house so there's not even a remote chance he could overhear what we'll be talking about.

"Sure. I'll go right now," Guy responds cheerfully. "Anything sounds good or you forget something, text me. You'll have plenty of time. I can never find my way around the grocery store. The Pentagon, no problem. Walmart, totally lost." We all three laugh as he picks up his wallet and keys. "Kate, thank you, again. I'll see you later." He kisses Brittany on the cheek and heads toward the door.

The minute the door shuts, my eyes turn back to Brittany's. Her face is unreadable—totally void of emotion.

"Why don't you come back to the baby's room where we can talk," Brittany says. I nod and move to follow her down the dark hallway.

Here you go, says the voice in my head.

Chapter Nine

A sleeping baby commands the energy in the room, and baby Kate is no exception. The room is decorated in varying shades of pink and is too perfect. There's what a new mom wants her nursery to look like, following a certain theme, and then there's what Brittany has done—what an American nursery is supposed to look like, but carefully void of all personality. I've been in a space like this before—John's ex-wife Clare's home. I dismiss these emotional memories immediately.

Baby Kate lies swaddled in a blush gauze blanket. Though just over five pounds, her small cheeks are chubby and the color of pink rose petals. She has a mop of reddish-brown hair that looks like her father's. Her eyelids are as delicate as tissue paper and I see her eyes move quickly back and forth underneath, perhaps dreaming her first dream in this new world. I want to cradle her in my arms and tell her how sorry I am that she's caught between two very different countries, but I can't. At least not right now.

My emotions stay in check, but they shift around, adjusting and gaining a different footing in this new space that baby Kate controls. Is this why Brittany chose to talk to me here, because she knew that the energy of this new life would throw me off? Brittany appears unaffected by the sleeping form of her new daughter. She walks directly to the baby monitor on the changing table and clicks it off and then turns and leans against it with her arms folded. We are the only ones in the house, but Brittany won't take any chances of someone hearing what she's about to say. I would have done the same thing. I sit down in a white rocking chair, allowing Brittany to remain standing in a position of dominance.

"She's beautiful," I say, letting my gaze rest on the sleeping baby. Brittany's eyes never leave my face and I feel them calculating everything I'm showing her. The silence expands from that of a normal conversational pause to the new reality that now exists between us. I turn my eyes to meet hers and work to keep a restrained look of hope on my face. What is she thinking? She's not giving up anything. Her eyes test mine for three long beats before she speaks.

"You know what I am, and yet I haven't been contacted for questioning. That's not the CIA they taught me about in Russia."

"I haven't talked to anyone about you . . . yet." Brittany's eyebrow flickers upward, a micro expression she allows me to see in response to the "yet." I need to be careful. If I'm too easy, she'll never trust me.

"What happens when the CIA finds out you knew about your neighbor who's a SVR agent and didn't tell them?" she asks.

"They trust me." I shrug my shoulders to imply that I'm willing to breach that trust. Baby Kate mews and squirms, then settles back into her slumber. Brittany doesn't even glance toward the bassinet.

"You *are* one to break the rules. At least you were with John's ex-wife, running ahead of your team into her house," she says.

Now it's my turn to raise an eyebrow. The incident she just described was in classified files. Brittany is showing me just how powerful and far-reaching the people are who control her. She's done a lot of homework in the last twenty-four hours. Or perhaps she learned all she could about her neighbors before she and Guy ever moved here. Russia is Russia, after all.

"I guess so," I say. The ball's still in her court. She needs to make her point.

She won't wait. She'll do it soon, says the voice in my head.

"So, what reason do you have to break the rules now, with me?" she asks. Now's the time, and I let the anger out. It quickens my heart rate and breathing, colors my cheeks, and darkens my eyes—all outward signs that I know Brittany is carefully logging into her mind.

"I have my reasons. They won't amount to much, though," I answer. I lift my narrowed eyes to meet hers. I clench my jaw and ball my hands into fists.

"What if I told you that there is a way to have it amount to something?" Brittany whispers. It's the first time she's lowered her voice since coming into the room where her child sleeps. I'm sure she's not whispering for her baby's benefit, but to add emphasis to her words.

"What do you mean?" I ask. I know exactly what she means, but I have to ask. I want her to say the words.

"You Americans are slaves to human connection. You let it drive your lives. My guess is that you spent your life hating your father, then you find out he just liked his job more than he liked you. And now you're angry. Am I right?"

Brittany has the first part right. I spent my life until last year hating my father. But he didn't put his job first. He left us to protect us, putting our safety before everything, even his broken heart. I don't know everything about my father, but I *know* he loved my mother, and he loves me.

This works. Go with it, says the voice in my head.

"What drives you?" I ask with a defensive edge to my voice. Her mouth slowly curves up into a smile.

"I'm connected to my country. Mother Russia drives me. We'll bring her back to the power she once was," Brittany says with fire in her eyes. My heart skips a beat at her use of the word "we." She could mean Putin, but my gut tells me she's referring to other sleeper cells like her, the ones I need to find.

"I don't believe in your country," I say with even more defensiveness.

"You don't need to. You just need a way to hurt yours. Your father was MI6. You weaken American intelligence, you weaken British intelligence, too. They're close allies." Relief tingles in my chest and I know it shows on my face. Brittany will think my relief comes from seeing a path for my revenge. But I indulge myself a second of this emotion because she believes my father is no longer with MI6, that he's out of the game. He's not, though, and he's hidden it so well that the Russians don't even know.

"I *do* want to hurt what he loved more than me. I want to damage it beyond repair. I *hate* James McLean and I want to ruin him. I want to see him suffer," I say. My jaw is clenched so tightly that the muscles in my neck are

THE PITCH

strained ropes. My hands are balled into white-knuckled fists, ready to hit someone. I want Brittany, and Russia, to believe that if my father were to walk into the room right now, I'd kill him. "And I do this by giving you our secrets," I say. It's not a question. Brittany's face pales, but her shoulders are set and her eyes focused on mine. I keep my truths behind a curtain and the anger front and center.

"That's exactly how you do it," she says. There are the words I've been waiting for—the pitch. I move my eyes to a spot on the wall just over her shoulder, as if I'm seeing a vision of my revenge, and the edges of my mouth lift to a slight grin.

"I'll want money, too. Eventually I'll need to run, and when I do, I want to do it comfortably," I say. Revenge is a viable reason to turn traitor, but greed is even more so. She wouldn't believe me if I didn't ask for money.

"You Americans and your need for things." She smirks and shakes her head. "We both know how this game works. I won't need to babysit you, so we can get down to business. But I'll need some bona fides and then we'll talk money." Brittany lets her eagerness show as she says this—her voice raises an octave and her words are rushed, almost falling over each other. She's right. She won't need to go through the normal months of vetting me that a double operation would require and for this, she's fortunate. She's got a cover to salvage, and she needs to do it now. This was quick, though. So much quicker than I imagined. It's as if someone has thrown me onto a speeding train I must control.

"Give me a couple of days, but I'll bring you something good," I say.

The front door opens and I hear keys drop on the kitchen counter. Guy is home. That was quick; he probably flew through the store wanting to get home to his wife and new daughter.

"A few days, then," she says with a finality that thuds in the pit of my stomach.

I've become a double agent.

Chapter Ten

"How did that Russian get into my files?" Gina says the minute I walk through my front door. As soon as Brittany told me what she knew about my rule breaking, I knew Gina would be furious. Gina and her tech team have created what they believe to be an unhackable system for our files. The news that someone has hacked their system won't go down well. Gina will take it as a personal assault.

"They're Russian. It's what they do," Maxwell says, looking even grumpier than before I left, if that's possible. John can barely contain his pride.

"You handled that perfectly. You're going to find this group of cells. You're going to do it," he says. I try to give him a determined nod, but it's really a weak swallow and a shrug. I turn to my team, who all show the eager determination I'm trying to fake.

"She didn't say one thing about her baby," Eva says.

"Because she's desperate," Denise says.

"She's Russian intelligence. It's what she does," Maxwell says.

"Whatever she is, I'm gonna find her little group along with everyone she ever said hi to," Gina says. "This just got way personal."

I smile at Gina and notice she has bright-pink reading glasses perched on the end of her nose. They match her bright-pink dangle earrings and the shade of lipstick she's wearing. Did I notice this before? She's been here for hours. My surroundings are clearer and closer. Self-doubt gives way to calm, and I exhale for what feels like the first time today. *The scripture in Isaiah applies to you, too*, says the voice in my head. *Trust the Lord and get to work.* My stomach rumbles with hunger but now I want to talk about everything.

"Do you mind if I eat something while we play the recording and I fill in the blanks?"

"Go ahead and start, and I'll make you a sandwich," Eva says. We spend the afternoon going through the recorded conversation, adding in body language, facial expressions, and what my gut was telling me. Thanks to Gina, we also have a copy of the 911 call I made with Brittany's Russian in the background. Denise's assessment was unanimously confirmed, even by Maxwell, that Brittany is desperate to keep her cover. There was also no question about how well Brittany has been trained.

"She's been trained since she could walk and talk," says Maxwell. "We didn't think Putin was playing these kinds of games, but he is. He's a sick son of a gun and he has no rules."

"You're right. So how do we play against someone who doesn't keep the rules? We know a little more a little sooner than they do," John says. "We find who Brittany's working with and stop them." We all nod. We have a lot of work ahead of us, beginning with a meeting with Audrey Brier first thing tomorrow morning. Brittany's pitch to me will be a top priority for counterintelligence. But tonight, I have a reprieve—dinner with John, Rose, and Livvy.

The weather in May can be precarious, but this evening is perfect—cool, clear, with low humidity. I'm not surprised to see that we'll be eating dinner outside in Rose's garden. It's a riot of color and the air is filled with the spicy sent of roses, lilies, and hyacinth.

Thoughts of self-doubt elbowed their way into my mind as I was getting ready this evening. Will I feel different around those I love, now that I've taken on this new role? How do I manage relationships in my real life when my double agent profile will take so much of my emotional energy? But these doubts melt away as I stand in Rose's garden. She's setting the table with the special occasion white linen table cloth and china. A vase of orange tulips graces the center of the table.

John tells his mom most of what he does at work, she being one of the few trusted people he can read into his work as a CIA officer. Clearly, he's already told Rose of my day and she's making tonight special to encourage me. Rose turns at the sound of my steps on the stone path and her face lights up.

Rose is slender and petite, with a youthful face that challenges the streaks of gray in her long, black hair that is pulled back and held by a silver clip. She's dressed in all white—a long skirt and knit sweater. She looks as she always does regardless of what she wears—elegant and understated. I wonder, like I have many times, how beautiful her Japanese mother must have been and long to have met her. Rose's eyes hold mine for a second before she pulls me into an embrace.

"Is *congratulations* the right word to use?" she whispers in my ear. The fountain is on, the fountain John put in the garden to mask the quiet conversations with his mom and now with me. Rose said nothing specific about my new operation because, like John, she will take every precaution. I pull away and allow her concerned expression to comfort me—she understands, she cares, she's there for me.

The agency always encourages officers to read in someone, usually a spouse, so there's someone in their life who really knows what they do. These trusted people are crucial to keeping those who work in espionage mentally and emotionally healthy. Despite what Brittany said, human connection is vital. Russian intelligence doesn't believe this. So how has Brittany done what she's done and kept the secrets she has? How often does she contact the other Russian SVR agents like her?

"You're here!" squeals Livvy. She runs through the open glass door and wraps her arms around my legs. She's dressed in a pink dress with a full skirt that flows with her every step. John walks up to the both of us, chuckling. One of the many joys of having a five-year-old in your life is that every time they see you, it's as if they haven't seen you in months instead of forty-eight hours ago, which is the last time I saw Livvy.

I kneel to fully embrace her, careful to not smash her long, dark ringlets that I assume were created by her father.

Her brown eyes are dancing with excitement and her smile, so much like her father's, fills her entire face.

"Dad said you got a special job today. That's why I get to dress up and we get to use the fancy dishes," Livvy says all in one breath. I glance up at John, who grins and gives me a quick wink. He's wearing his dark dress pants and white shirt from work but has no tie, and his shirt sleeves are rolled up. I don't feel so under dressed in my tan capris and white sweater.

"I did. Thank you. You look especially lovely tonight," I say. Livvy beams with excitement and twirls to show me her dress in motion.

We eat roast with new potatoes and carrots from Rose's garden followed by strawberry shortcake. We slowly enjoy our food as the sun goes down, talking about small, unimportant things—nothing to do with my special job. Thankfully, Livvy doesn't ask questions for now, happy to just have a reason to celebrate.

I've often wondered what soldiers do the night before an engagement with the enemy. How do they prepare? I'm sure every soldier has their own way of facing the battle. For me, this evening is perfect—a generous dose of ordinary life. It grounds and steadies me, putting me on even footing for what the coming weeks may bring. John knows I need this evening and, thanks to Rose, made it happen. I love them both for it. I'm in their circle, like the necklace around my neck represents. Will it all stay like this after tomorrow?

After Livvy finishes eating, she wanders into the house and I see her at the table with her drawing pad and crayons, satisfying a sudden need to color something.

"How are you really doing?" Rose asks in a lowered voice. John is sitting to my right and reaches over to rub his thumb across the back of my hand. It's a simple gesture and one he's done many times, but right now it sends warmth up my arm that rolls into my chest. I'm surprised at how much I need the connection his touch brings me. Am I more aware of my connection to others because of what Brittany said to me about Americans being addicted to it? I'm certainly more aware of how I'll handle assets in the future.

"I'm okay one minute and then a little shaky the next. I have a lot more compassion for what I've asked my assets to do, that's for sure," I answer. Though this situation with Brittany is unique, I'm still sitting on the other side of the asset-handler desk.

"I felt that way," John says. "It made me a better handler. We're going to take it one step at a time. Each operation has its own course and goes at its own pace."

"We're always here for you when you need a break. You'll have people watching you—you probably already do—but no one will question you coming over here," Rose says. I swallow and nod in thanks. Not every spy has support like this.

I didn't feel Livvy come up, but suddenly she puts a drawing on the table in front of me.

"You'll have to travel for your special job, right? Here's a picture of you on a plane going to your special job," she says. The drawing is of an airplane, my face in the window. Like she always draws me, I have long, dark hair and light-blue eyes. Clouds surround the plane and a large orange sun smiles from the top right-hand corner of the paper. I look at John for a second, allowing him to see the hand of fear that grips my stomach and wrings it like a wet towel.

The job of a successful double agent will involve providing Brittany and her SVR handler with carefully chosen intel that proves I am a trustworthy and viable agent without harming American intelligence. If my trust ever comes into question, I will be eliminated—in other words, killed. They can't, of course, eliminate me on American soil because it would draw too much unwanted attention. My elimination would come as an invitation to Russia, to meet with some people Brittany works for. If I get on an airplane for this operation, it could be the last thing I do. I quickly draw a curtain in front of this fear and then turn to look at Livvy.

"This is a great picture. If I have to fly on an airplane, I'll take it with me so I can remember you," I say. Livvy smiles a smile that fills her eyes, and bounces on her tip toes.

"Okay, Livvy, time for bed," Rose says. I don't know how much Rose understands about the dangers of my new operation, but I sense she picked up on the vibe and is trying to arrange some privacy for John and me. Rose tells us to leave the dishes for later and takes an unenthusiastic Livvy through the glass door, shuts it, and draws the curtains across it. John stands and pulls me up with him.

"Let's go sit by the fountain," he says.

The splash of water on rocks is normally soothing to me, but the twisting fear in my stomach dominates the effects of the fountain. The fountain's real purpose is to allow conversations like the one John and I are about to have—two spies speaking freely.

"I won't let you get on a plane to Russia," John says as soon as we sit down on the bench.

"What if that's the only way I can find out who Brittany's working with? What if it goes that far?" I ask.

"You have a great team of people working with you behind the scenes. With a few pieces of key information, we'll be able to find out what we need," he says. I turn so I can look at him full on and hold his eyes with mine. From the garden lights I can see his eyes—dark, exotic, and always safe, which is why I'm allowing my eyes to ask him the questions I don't want to verbalize. What if we aren't enough? What if we are no match against the Russians? What if they see who I really am and Brittany and her cell go dark, never to be found again?

John pulls me to him and I rest my head on his shoulder. I feel the beat of his heart and the even rise and fall of his chest. His shirt has the faint smell of his clean-smelling cologne, even after a day's work.

I curl tighter into his embrace. There are no answers to the questions my eyes asked him and we both know it. So, he offers me what he can, the comfort of his physical protection and his love.

"We'll take this a step at a time. We won't be able to see the end from the beginning. But we have to remember that we're doing this to stop some serious evil. You've done that before, just not this way," John says. I nod against his chest, then pull away and seek the safety of his eyes again.

"I've already felt the peace that Isaiah talks about in the scripture you shared with us. It would be nice to have that peace all the time," I say. John smiles, but the smile stays on his lips and doesn't move up into his eyes.

"You'll have the peace when you need it most," he says.

He's right, says the voice in my head.

John takes my face in his hands and kisses me—a tender, reassuring kiss. It's followed by another, and then another, each kiss becoming more urgent, as if our time is short. I pull away, breathy and concerned.

"This will stay the same, right? We'll stay the same?" I ask. John smiles again, and this time it reaches his eyes.

"It will stay the same. After tonight, we may have some Russians watching us, but I'm good if you are," he says. Two beats follow and then we both burst out laughing. We appreciate well-timed spy humor.

The light in Livvy's bedroom goes out and, still laughing, we both get up to help Rose with the dishes.

Chapter Eleven

Audrey Brier is leaning back in her chair with her legs stretched out straight in front of her. Her arms are relaxed, lying on the armrests of her chair. She could just as easily be on a beach somewhere, watching the tide come in instead of waiting to question me about becoming a double agent.

Officer Brier looks me in the eye and smiles as I stand on the other side of the conference table. She wears dark pants and a white long-sleeved blouse. Her shoulder-length sandy-blonde hair is pulled back and held with a clip. She wears no jewelry and little makeup yet looks nicely put together. She commands the room in a powerful but simple way and I feel instantly calmed by it. I offer a quick prayer of gratitude because I would not be feeling this way if Norman Steele were sitting here.

"Officer Ross, it's nice to finally meet you," Officer Brier says. She stands and motions me to come to her side of the table. We are the only two in the conference room, but I know John and the team are coming. I assumed Officer Brier would want me positioned across the table from her so she could assess me, but on her cue, I walk around and extend my hand. Her grip is firm and her green eyes are engaging and kind. Not, like some officers, stoically distant in a professionally prescribed way.

"It's nice to meet you," I reply.

"Please, call me Audrey. And may I call you Kate?" she asks.

"Of course," I answer. Power hungry Norman Steele would have had me salute him if he thought he could get away with it. I need to quit comparing Audrey to him. She's making her position as head of counterintelligence her own in a warm, approachable way, and it's nice for a change.

"Please sit down. I've asked everyone else to come a little later so I could visit privately with you," she says. This explains why no one else is here. I couldn't imagine John and my team being late for such an important meeting.

We both sit, our chairs slightly turned to face each other. Audrey is thin in an athletic way. She looks much younger than her fifty-five years and, in some ways, reminds me of Rose—genetically blessed to look youthful no matter her age.

"I'm up to speed on where you're at with Brittany. This is quite the operation you've stumbled onto. How are you feeling about all of this?" Before I can stop them, my eyes widen with surprise at such a personal question right off the bat.

"Well, I . . ." I start to answer but pause.

"Kate, I'm not Norman Steele," Audrey says and smiles. My eyebrows raise as high as they'll go, and I chuckle.

"No, you are most definitely *not* Norman Steele," I say.

"You've been thrown into an operation you've never done before, something most officers train a long time for.

THE PITCH

I'm going to help you through this and help your team help you." "So, how are you feeling?" she asks again. I exhale and drop my shoulders. Neal likes Audrey and I see why.

"Overwhelmed. I feel overwhelmed. I'm afraid Brittany will see through me, and she and whoever else she's working with will disappear." Audrey nods in agreement.

"Of course you are. I would be. You need to remember that all your tradecraft will apply to this double agent operation just like it did when you were a case officer. You'll just rely more heavily on instinct with this one." I wince at the memory of Nahla and how my instinct failed her, but I set the memory aside. I have to look forward.

"I'll remember that," I say.

"You've already had encounters with her. Tell me what your mind produced to protect you from showing the truth." My eyebrows come together, unsure of what she's asking.

"I'm not sure what you mean," I say. She smiles and leans forward in an encouraging manner.

"From what I hear, you have an incredible instinct. You *are* James McLean's daughter, after all. Your instinct will bring images into your mind that will help you safely maneuver through some tricky encounters. What were those images?"

I understand her question now but curl my lips in, still unsure of allowing Audrey into my mind. Does a spy as good as my father rely on mental images of stages and curtains? But if Neal trusts Audrey, then I can, too.

"A couple of images came to my mind. One where I was standing on a stage, only allowing certain thoughts and emotions to be in front of the curtain. And another of walking barefoot across a stable surface. I wasn't sure if the floor was steady, but as I moved forward, I learned it was."

"That's great. Perfect. Perhaps the stage-and-curtain image can help you with your exchanges with Brittany, helping you know what to show her and what to keep behind the curtain. The image of walking on solid ground was probably very reassuring," she says.

"It was. But shouldn't I have something sturdier than a curtain? That feels a little flimsy. I'm sure Brittany hides her secrets behind a mental block wall."

"I'm sure she does. And how long do you think it would take her to break down that block wall to get to what's real? If she's even able to?" Audrey asks. I've been so concerned about hiding the truth from Brittany, I have given little thought to the wisest way to do it.

"I haven't really looked at it from that angle."

"As flimsy as that curtain may feel, you always have the power to open and close it, and decide what's behind it and what's on stage for others to see. You want what's real easy to get to. If Brittany has been trained from childhood, which I'm certain she has been, she's had everything real about herself well blocked off," she says.

"But the real Brittany came through. Childbirth saw to that," I say.

"That's right, and she was completely unprepared for it. Soviet intelligence believes they can remove a person's identity completely. But that's impossible. Who you are will always come through. Something will always trigger it. So, you need to prepare for it," she says.

She's right, says the voice in my head. I wince at the thought of being so exposed to my enemy.

"It's hard to imagine being so taken off guard. I don't know how many times I've thought of the almost impossible tasks I've asked my assets to perform," I say.

"This operation will make you a better case officer. I'm sure you've heard that, though." I nod.

"I'll help you prepare for such a moment. But what's crucial is you see your true identity as a strength in your role as an intelligence officer, not as a weakness. I understand you are a woman of faith, so you'll understand when I say that we are hardwired for truth—to recognize it and identify with it. God created us this way," she says.

"I believe that, though it can be a conflict of interest in our line of work if we don't keep our 'why' always in front of us," I say.

"You're right. We have to be willing to take our 'why' into the shadows to find the truth. You'll really be tested on that with this operation. Another tremendous strength you have is your relationships. Our need for connection is God-given and a strength, though Soviet intelligence will claim the opposite, as Brittany has already told you. Your relationships will save you, which is why you need to keep them behind an easily accessed curtain, not a block wall," she says. *She's right again*, says the voice in my head.

Audrey *is* right. My heart lifts at her words.

"So, how do I do all of this?" I ask. There's a light tap at the door and John sticks his head in. He gives me a quick smile and then looks at Audrey and says, "You ready for us?"

"Yes," she says to John, then answers my question in a whisper.

"Your relationships will save you, and here comes your saviors right now."

Chapter Twelve

The thumb drive is small and white. It lies in the palm of my hand and disappears when I close my fist around it. It contains what the intelligence community calls my bona fides—a classified information offering that will convince Russian intelligence that I will be a viable agent for them.

A double agent operation is a pay-to-play game—if I don't pay up with some actionable intelligence, the Russians will suspect I'm exactly what I am, a double agent. Many officers worked around the clock the past two days to come up with what's on this thumb drive. The Russians are too smart to hand botched-together, doctored intel that is of no worth to them. But they will be suspicious of something too spectacular, considering I had just a few days to "steal" it. What I give Brittany has to be the real deal and believable under the circumstances.

Some officers above my pay grade had to decide if it's worth it to sacrifice what I hold in my hand—the location of a CIA safehouse in Moscow. Of course, the Moscow station and any activity on our part surrounding this safehouse will be convincingly staged. But considering the extremely high level of surveillance the SVR puts on anything American in their country, this is a substantial loss. Even if no Americans are captured at this safe house, which I pray they won't be, it will still be a win for the Russians with the time it will take the CIA to establish another safe house. Brittany's SVR handler should be very pleased with this little white thumb drive.

Audrey spent the rest of the afternoon yesterday with John, the team, and me, going over operational details, security protocols, and some potential scenarios to work through. Our overall goal is to keep giving Brittany valuable feed material in order to gain her trust and move me up in the eyes of her superiors. We want Brittany to feel safe enough with me to give us a clue about who she's working with.

Brittany's people will have constant surveillance on my home, and they may try to enter and plant a bug. Just in case, I'll have equipment to detect any kind of recording or tracking device in my home and vehicle. I'll also be scanned before entering headquarters.

Brittany will always suspect me of betrayal in the form of recording devices—anyone running a double agent operation would—so she'll be constantly watching for any new items of clothing or jewelry I wear. My microphone will either be on familiar jewelry or a ponytail holder—all items Brittany has seen me wear many times. She will pay close attention to my cell phone, so I'll make a show of turning it off in front of her. She won't do the same for me, though. But this is how it works—I'm proving to her and the SVR that I'm a legitimate traitor. Brittany needs to believe she's running this operation.

"It's important that your exchanges with Brittany aren't too scripted. Spontaneity will always come across as

THE PITCH

genuine as opposed to something you've practiced. Trust your gut. Rely on the strengths of your team to analyze the exchanges and pick apart any details. But in the moment, let your instinct call the shots," Audrey counseled me. Audrey will keep the feed material coming but I'll decide, along with my team, when I hand it over to Brittany. I'm a nervous CIA officer seeking revenge by stealing classified intel. This process should look like an uncertain trajectory on my part.

Today, though, is a definitive step forward by giving Brittany my bona fides. Brittany took baby Kate on a short walk by herself yesterday evening at six. This is a little soon to be taking a newborn out, but she might be creating an opportunity for us to meet. If she does the same today, I'll know it's a sign that I can join her for a private exchange. In the world of espionage, a consistent schedule and routine are done on purpose.

At six sharp, the Halls' garage door lifts and Brittany comes out pushing a baby stroller. The evening is clear but still carries the humidity of a warm, sticky afternoon. I put the thumb drive in the pocket of my denim shorts. I'm wearing a white tank top and sandals. The microphone is on a plastic claw clip that holds my hair up off my neck. I quickly text headquarters that I'm meeting Brittany and then open my front door.

As Brittany pushes the stroller down her driveway, she sees me and waves. I look like any neighbor chancing upon a new mom taking her baby for a walk. Of course, I'll want to visit so I can ask how the new mom is managing and see the baby. No situation could look more normal—there's nothing suspicious about what's playing out in front of our homes. Yet, this is how espionage happens. Rarely is the gathering of intel and the selling of secrets accomplished like it is in the movies.

I wave back to Brittany and smile. As I walk toward her, I allow the many questions I have regarding her to roll through my mind. How much does she know about me? How well is she trained? Russian intelligence trains their people differently than we do, but Brittany and I are both spies. So, what's the crossover of trade craft? I allow the energy and nuance of these questions to surround me and show on my face, as they should. After all, I'm a CIA officer about to sell my first secret to the Russians... on the street in front of my house.

"Beautiful evening for a walk," I say. Brittany smiles and nods, but her tired, dark-ringed eyes are carefully assessing me. This first exchange between us is a make-it-or-break-it moment for our arrangement. I could have the FBI waiting to swarm her and take her in for questioning. The fear of that happening must have been living rent free in her brain for the past few days. But if this exchange goes off without a hitch, which it will, I will have earned a bit more confidence with her.

I bend over to look at baby Kate. She is snug asleep, wrapped in a cream-colored receiving blanket. Gina's choice to put my bona fides on a white thumb drive was inspired—it will blend in perfectly since baby Kate will play an important part in this exchange.

I take my phone out of my back pocket and pretend to be taking a picture of baby Kate, but I turn the phone so Brittany can see that I'm turning it off. She gives me a quick nod of approval.

"I won't need to train you on much," Brittany says quietly.

"There'll probably be some things you'll have to tell me. We are from two very different organizations," I say. I want her to talk to me as much as possible, even if it's repeating protocols I already know. The most basic information can contain a lead.

I slide my phone back into my pocket and reach for the thumb drive, but stop. *Not yet*, says the voice in my head. I pull my hand out empty, something that doesn't go unnoticed by Brittany.

I stand fully up and meet Brittany's searching gaze. I'm visibly nervous and frightened and the emotions are genuine—handing over a safe house to a Russian spy is working for me on all levels. Fear is hard to fake. *Walk for a few moments. Get her talking*, says the voice in my head.

I turn my body in the direction the stroller is facing and motion for us to walk. Brittany's eyes are pinched and her mouth is a straight line. Like me, she's been trained that the slightest change in my mood could mean trouble—she appears acutely aware of every nuance. I would do the same.

"You have the bona fides, right?" she asks. I take a deep breath and nod.

"I have them. They're in my pocket."

We walk in silence for about thirty seconds. Two cars drive past, both men in our neighborhood coming home from work. Neither acknowledges us. Both men look tired, their gazes locked on the road in front of them.

"Not having second thoughts, are you?" Brittany asks with an edge of sarcasm. I don't turn to look at her, but I can sense the fear she's trying to mask.

"No," I say, "It's just a . . ." Adrenalin fires up my neck and burns into my jaw. The sound of heavy, quick footsteps pounds up behind us.

Chapter Thirteen

"There you are," Guy says. He's in his Pentagon-pressed work clothes, though his tie falls loose and his shirt is slightly untucked. He's red faced and perspiring from the one-block run from his home. Brittany's pale and wide eyed but recovers quickly.

"Hey, you're home early. We just thought we'd take a little walk," Brittany says, smiling down at baby Kate. Guy misses whatever adrenalin-fueled energy that's floating around. He focuses his attention solely on his daughter.

"That's great," he says, his eyes sweeping the stroller. He reaches in and runs his fingers gently over her head, then lays the palm of his hand on her stomach—perhaps subconsciously assuring himself that she's alive and breathing. If I would have tucked the thumb drive into her blanket a few minutes ago like I'd planned to, Guy would have felt it. I offer a quick prayer of gratitude for the voice in my head.

"I didn't mean to worry you," Brittany says to Guy, who's still flushed and sweaty. Guy laughs and wipes his brow with his shirtsleeve.

"I guess I'm just being a nervous first-time father. I got home, and no one was there, so I assumed the worst," he says. He gives me a sheepish smile and shrugs. "Okay. I'm a weirdo. What I can I say?" We all laugh at his confession, but my heart sags at the horrible secrets hidden from him. He'll learn all of them soon enough. For right now, he's being a typical over-protective father—protecting his daughter from the dangers his imagination creates. I'm certain "Russian spy mom" hasn't entered his mind. Brittany turns the stroller around and we head back toward our homes.

"So, how *are* you doing?" I ask Guy. "Are either of you getting any sleep?"

"Snatches here and there. It's not too bad," Brittany says.

"I'm supposed to have some time off, but there's some stuff going on at work. Doesn't look like I'll be able to take any days for a while. You would not believe the amount of coffee I drank today to stay awake," Guy says.

Brittany and Guy are to my left and when I glance over at them. My chest tightens and I fold my arms. As Guy chatters on about how busy it was at work, Brittany has a grin on her face that looks as if she'd hit the mother lode of intel. If Guy caught his wife's grin, he probably thought she was proud of her hard-working, dependable husband. But what my gut tells me is that Brittany's delighted that "there's some stuff going on at the Pentagon" and she's gathering a ton of intel off her exhausted, distracted husband. How is she doing it? Bugs? Hacking? What does Guy bring home from work? It's been quite the week for Russian spy Brittany Hall—turning a CIA officer and making a major haul off her Pentagon-employed husband.

We stop in front of the Halls' house and the appropriate thing for me to do is say goodbye and head home—the sun has dipped below the horizon and baby Kate is squirming.

But I wait a minute, giving Brittany one more chance to get my bona fides.

"Honey, will you go turn the sprinklers on? I was going to earlier and forgot," Brittany says to Guy. He nods and heads off around the side of their house.

"Now," Brittany says to me and holds out her hand. Her eyes are narrow and her lips are pursed—she looks like she's had it and would like this exchange to be over. I wonder just how much she told her superiors. Do they know how completely she blew her cover? Regardless, they couldn't have been happy about the vulnerable position she's put them in. They've probably been pressuring her like crazy for the bona fides. A rhythmic thrum fills the air and the sprinklers come to life.

"Here," I say and hand her the thumb drive, then made the exchange look like I was giving Brittany's hand a comforting squeeze because Guy appears from the side of the house. I give him a quick wave, turn, and head toward my house. Brittany's hand was cold and clammy. I carefully wipe my hand across the front of my tank top so neither can see me doing it.

I was tailed on my way to headquarters this morning. I describe the car—a gray Chevy Impala with tinted windows—to John and the team. No one is surprised.

"You can't look back," John says. "This is one of those times you have to let them watch you."

"I know. All they saw was normal mirror checking," I say.

"Y'all, it seems like such a cat-and-mouse game," Gina says, and she's right. She's hunched over her laptop. Black reading glasses adorned with rhinestone flowers sit on the end of her nose, and as I feared, a can of Red Bull with her bright-red lipstick marks sits next to her laptop. When Gina goes deep on an operation, she resorts to Red Bull to pull some long hours. No one can deny, though, that the drink has saved us, especially me.

"It is. But it's one the Russians want to play. They know Kate knows they're going to watch her. But she's now officially an agent for their country, so she has to put up with their protocols," John says.

"Speaking of protocol, no one entered my house while I made the exchange yesterday evening, and so far, no tracking devices have been put on my car," I say. "Just a Russian following me to work." I wanted so badly to call John when I got home last night, but I couldn't take the chance. Though I was exhausted after my "walk" with Brittany, I got little sleep, worrying about the safe house. Would someone be compromised by what I sacrificed? Will I be able to find out who Brittany is working with so all this will be worth it?

I took John and the team through the exchange with Brittany—they had already listened to the recording, so I filled in the details.

"I was just about to express some fear to Brittany, letting her know this was a big step for me, in hopes it would get her talking to assure me, when I heard footsteps coming toward us," I say.

"I bet you felt like you were having a heart attack when you heard Guy running toward you," Eva says.

"But nothing like what Brittany was feeling," Denise says. "For all she knew, he could have been the FBI coming to haul her off."

"You're right. She was stressed, for sure, but she covered it pretty well. Guy didn't pick up on anything."

"Guy said there was 'some stuff' going on at the Pentagon. That's why he couldn't take any time off?" John asks. I press my lips together and nod.

"And Brittany seemed pretty pleased with it. I really want to know how she's getting intel from him," I say.

"Oh, you better believe I'm working on it," Gina says. She hasn't stopped typing since I walked into the conference room. "I'm gonna find out everything there is to know about Miss Brittany." Gina punctuates this statement with a big gulp of Red Bull. We all wince but say nothing.

"Nice work following your instinct and not putting the thumb drive in the baby's blanket," Denise says. I raise my eyebrows and nod.

"The thumb drive wouldn't have been visible because it was the same color as her blanket," I say. Gina stops typing long enough to give me an air high five. "But Guy would have felt it. And that would have been hard to explain away, no matter how tired and distracted he was."

"It's nerve-racking, but you can't plan for stuff like Guy surprising you. You just have to prepare yourself to be in tune with your instinct," Denise says. She speaks from experience, having seen her way through many surprises on the streets of New York.

"You're right," Johns says. "As hard as it is, keep still inside and listen."

There's a light tap on the door and Audrey Brier comes in. My mouth goes dry despite the watery sensation of saliva pooling up in the back of my throat. This reaction isn't from Audrey herself—she brings her calming, commanding presence. It's what news she brings.

"We just got word from the Moscow station. No one was compromised when the safe house was seized." I blow air out of my mouth and rest my face in my hands. John, who's sitting next to me, leans over and gives my shoulder a squeeze. "A couple of American officers led the Russians on a believable chase, but they got away," Audrey adds.

"Thanks for telling me," I say, smiling and light-headed with relief. Audrey holds my eyes and returns the smile.

"Good work. It looks like you're in," she says. She sets a white thumb drive on the table and slides it across to me. I slap my hand down on top of it to stop it. "Here's your next feed material. There's also an offshore account where Brittany can send your payments."

A weight drops in the pit of my stomach. I have to do this all over again.

Chapter Fourteen

"Here ya go," Jake says and hands me a flat vacuumed-packed plastic bag. Jake is the best disguise guy at headquarters and what he just handed me is a quick-change disguise—items that allow me to completely change my profile in a matter of seconds no matter where I'm at, even walking down a busy sidewalk. I'll keep this bag with me at all times as one of many safety precautions. Though I have the thumb drive with the next feed material to hand over to Brittany, it's too soon to give it to her. She needs to believe I'm painstakingly gathering this feed material, which will take some time. In the meantime, the team and I have something else planned for this afternoon and it's important that I have a quick-change in my purse.

"Thanks. You're the best," I say. Jake smiles and shrugs. He just turned twenty-six but will probably always look much younger. He's thin and pale, with bright red hair and just recently added a mustache to his look, perhaps to appear closer to his age. Instead, he looks like a fifteen-year-old playing with facial hair. I will not be the one to tell him this, though. He'll eventually figure it out.

"I thought you'd probably need some more cover-up, too," he says. He hands me a small container filled with what looks like tan putty. Jake invented what I call his magic cover-up after my face was burned with a chemical weapon, leaving an easily identifiable scar—something no spy wants. Jake's cover-up completely hides the scar. He's promised to keep me stocked with it, a promise he's kept. I nod and curl my fingers around the profile-saving cream.

"I do. I'm almost out. I wish you'd let me pay you for this," I say. He's never accepted payment for this extra service.

"Not a chance," he says, and the familiar red blush creeps up his face. I don't push my offer but give him something that won't embarrass him but he won't refuse, either.

"Well, your lunch will be ready soon. It's your favorite. Starbucks will call you when it's ready," I say. Jake loves the panini sandwiches at Starbucks. Headquarters has a secret Starbucks that you won't find on any GPS and all the baristas have to pass rigorous background checks to work there. It's not surprising that it's the busiest Starbucks in the country. When I went to get Jake's lunch, they were running behind and promised to call Jake when his sandwich and Frappuccino were ready.

"Awesome. Thanks. And don't worry, you'll never recognize Denise out there in the wild," he adds. I chuckle and nod.

"I'm sure I won't," I say and then head back to my office.

My afternoon will be out in the wild, on the street "running errands." What I'm really doing is trying to get photographs of the Russian SVR surveillance team that have been following me around.

I'll be going to some usual spots I go to weekly—dry cleaners, bank, grocery store. All these locations are on one street in Kensington, close to my home. I usually park

THE PITCH

at the grocery store, walk to the dry cleaners and bank, then get my groceries last. Gina and Eva will split up in vans, each on an end of the block. They'll have tech guys with them and access to drones if they need them. The goal is to get photos or video footage of who's following me to see if they are in our database. If we know these Russians, their backgrounds could give us a clue who Brittany's working with.

Denise will be on foot and in a disguise I haven't seen. It's crucial I don't recognize any of my team, and that the Russians don't see any of my team watching them. Let the cat-and-mouse games begin.

What we're attempting with my "errand running" is risky—my cover as a double agent could be blown if one of my team is spotted. But Gina and Eva will be in service vans for the local cable company—not an unusual sight on the streets of Kensington. And Denise is an expert at blending into her surroundings—she knows how to be invisible.

I won't have any comms or an earpiece. I've been trained to read lips and we assume that Brittany and her people are as well. If they catch me talking to one of my team through comms, it will be a dead giveaway. But if we can get video footage of an SVR agent talking, I can read their lips off the video and maybe get a name.

It took some fast talking on my part to convince Maxwell to let the operation "running errands" happen without him. He wasn't happy about it but finally admitted that the fewer people around me, the better. We're breaking the rules, but what we could uncover—a Russian sleeper cell operating on US soil—is worth it.

I sit at my desk and take a deep breath. So much is at risk, and at the bottom of it all, like a heavy weight in the pit of my stomach, is an innocent baby and her father. I look out the window and see the vibrant green of late May. Though a little sticky, early summer can be beautiful in DC. I offer a prayer of gratitude that it's a beautiful, cloudless day. Weather won't blur any drone footage we get.

I turn and look at the doorway. John's standing there. I knew he was. I can sense when he's near—I feel the pull of him like a magnet. This is one reason he won't be playing a visible part this afternoon. It would be too distracting if I saw him. Another reason is that John never goes with me on these errands. Everything in my life needs to appear as normal as possible. Having John suddenly join me this afternoon would be a major red flag to Brittany. John will stay back here at headquarters, listening to comms and watching the drone footage.

"The team is in place and ready when you are," he says. I give him a grin, but it's half-hearted.

"I just have to run a few simple errands and pretend I don't have a circus going on around me," I say. His eyes soften and do something I love—cover my face with kisses. I take another deep breath as he comes toward me. Discreetly, he brushes my hand with his.

"No one can hold it together in the middle of a surveillance circus better than you. Let your mind be at peace and let your team do their jobs," he says. I give him a believable smile this time.

"Gotta go run some errands," I say.

Chapter Fifteen

I've had too much training to not feel the eyes on me. The same gray Impala follows me from headquarters to the Safeway grocery store by my house. As they have so far, they follow typical protocol when tailing a car—stay back a few cars and keep a steady speed. I didn't give them any challenges, letting them get comfortable. Maybe a drone can get a picture of the driver.

I park in the Safeway parking lot and head to the cleaners next door. Just out of habit, I keep my phone in my pocket and notice those around me. A distracted person is an easy target.

Today, though, it would be easier to have my head in my phone. Anything to ease this invasion of my world—an invasion I'm supposed to pretend doesn't exist.

There's a man standing outside the dry cleaners smoking. He's looking away from me, so I take in his appearance. I've never seen him before and make a list of his features—six feet, overweight, burn mark on his right hand, graying hair, acne scars on his neck. The most noticeable aspects of his appearance, though, have nothing to do with his physical features. He's holding his cigarette and standing like a European, not an American. Europeans usually stand with their weight evenly distributed between both legs, slightly arching their backs. Americans will commonly shift their weight from one leg to the other, having one hip jutted out. Europeans hold their cigarettes with their thumb and first finger, where most Americans will slide the cigarette between their first and second fingers. These are slight differences and may mean nothing—the DC area is a travel destination for people across the globe. But for me, today, a European standing outside my dry cleaners is enough for me to notice.

The smoke of the man's cigarette fills my lungs as I walk past him and I cough. My lungs don't tolerate smoke like they used to. His cigarette has the sickly-sweet smell of a cigar as opposed to the chemical smell of cigarettes. I'm afraid he'll turn and look at me, but he doesn't. I know he knows I'm here, though. I can feel it.

Marion, who always helps me at the cleaners, greets me and asks how I am. We talk for a minute and I watch as her eyes glance over my shoulder. Most people would follow her gaze to see what diverts her attention—a quick turn of the head mid-conversation. Despite all my training, I still fight the urge to look back. You can't ever look back.

I'm certain the smoking man outside is watching us through the glass front of the store. Marion's eyes glance over my shoulder again, and her eyebrows come together. I hand her my dry-cleaning ticket and her focus returns to me. I pay with my credit card and while I'm working the machine, Marion glances out the front window again. Her face is puzzled but clears when the machine chimes for me to remove my card. I take the receipt from her and the clothes she hands me—dark jackets, skirts, and pants—what Gina calls ugly agency suits.

Marion and I say our goodbyes and as I turn to leave, I see the smoking man's body quickly turn to face away from me. He's awkward and obvious—hardly the Russian-level surveillance I was expecting. At least he's making it easy for my team to photograph him, though I have his profile down by now. If he stays with me for the rest of my errands, I'll be able to draw his face myself.

I hang my dry cleaning in my car and walk through the parking lot to the bank. I don't allow my eyes to find the smoking man on the sidewalk, but I feel him. He's orbiting me. I wait behind two people to use the outside ATM, and when it's my turn, my lungs fill with the smoke from the smoking man's cigarette. He's behind me. All it would take is for my eyes to glance upward once into the ATM's security mirror and he'd be blown . . . and so would I. He knows it and he knows I know it. So, I complete my transaction, breathing in the acrid smell of smoke while he blatantly watches me. Denise is out here somewhere. I can't wait to hear what she thinks of this guy and his lousy surveillance tactics.

I put my bank card, receipt, and cash into my wallet, turn, and head back through the parking lot. I want to be away from this man. But I'm a Russian agent and they own me. They have to make sure I'm legit.

The grocery store looks busy and there are a lot of shopping carts in the parking lot. Rather than get inside the store and find out there aren't any shopping carts inside—forcing me to turn around and go back into the parking lot to retrieve one—I grab an abandoned one in a parking space. I don't want to have to turn abruptly around right now because I know smoking man is close behind me. I can still smell his smoke. Will he sacrifice his cigarette and follow me into the store that doesn't allow smoking, or let me shop in peace?

The automatic doors slide open and I inhale a deep breath of fruit and flowers—I entered by the produce and floral department. With a few more breaths, my lungs are clear of the cigarette smoke. I take my time looking at the flowers, then move onto the produce section. I don't feel the smoking man near me. *He waits for you outside*, says the voice in my head. Relief tingles through me and my shoulders drop. Is this what it will be like every time I go somewhere?

The aisles of Safeway are a familiar refuge for an hour. I don't rush, taking my time deciding the few items I need. Will I outwait the smoking man? Or is his only concern tailing me?

I finally check out and leave the store through the same doors I entered. The air quickly turns from fruity florals to smoking man's particular brand of cigarette. I could sniff this guy out anywhere. He's not trying very hard to blend in, that's for sure.

I load my groceries and head home. The gray Impala stays two cars back the whole way to my house. As I pull into my garage, he drives past. It's all I can do to not smile and wave.

I only get half of my groceries put away before I have to stop because my hands are shaking so badly. Despite all my preparation to take on the role of a double agent, nothing quite prepares you for the not knowing. Was someone on my team spotted by the Russians? I'm certain Gina and Eva got pictures of the smoking man, but is he in a database? Does his identity give us a clue? And if so, is there a lead to follow?

I want nothing more than to call headquarters to find out, but I can't. Even though I've stuck strictly to protocol, and as far as I know, I'm not bugged, I have to assume the Russians are listening and watching. I can't get in my car and go back to headquarters, not after I was so blatantly followed by smoker man—why would I if, according to the Russians, headquarters knows nothing of my deception? And I usually never do. Once I get groceries, I'm done for the day.

The last time I saw my father, he told me to have no obvious routines—always change the routes I drive and the places I go. He warned me that the people who are chasing him could watch me and a dependable routine would make me an easy target. But I don't think he ever considered I'd become a double agent, where predictability would be necessary. I'm sure my father would understand this. How I wish I could talk to him right now. How does he handle the not knowing?

Trust in the Lord. He will bring peace to your mind, says the voice in my head. I take a deep breath, and then clench and unclench my hands. The best way to keep my team and myself safe is to not know right now—to wait until I go to headquarters tomorrow to get some answers.

The four pints of rocky road ice cream are getting soft. I focus on putting the rest of my groceries away.

Chapter Sixteen

John is waiting for me this morning, just inside the door of headquarters. He knows it was a rough night of not knowing and he doesn't want me to go a second longer than I have to. I love him for this.

"We weren't spotted, and we don't have an ID on the guy that was following you," he says. I look at John and exhale, but I can't bring myself to smile. I'm grateful no one got caught, but I was so hoping we'd gather some kind of lead.

John and I remain silent as we work our way through security and I'm scanned for bugs. Gratefully, no one gets on the elevator with us and we can speak freely.

"You accomplished a lot yesterday," John says, as if he read my mind. I give him a look that clearly shows I don't agree with him. "You didn't look back, which proved to them you mean business. There aren't many trained operatives who would put up with what you put up with yesterday," he says.

I mouth a *thank you* to John as we enter the conference room. It looks like the team got an early start this morning. Guilt twists my stomach at the dark circles under their eyes. Everyone has a Starbucks cup next to them, and Gina is typing like crazy on her laptop with two cans of Red Bull next to her. She has on large kelly green hoop earrings and neon-green reading glasses that clash horribly. This combination seems surprisingly unplanned for Gina, which concerns me as much as the Red Bull. She gives me a quick smile and keeps typing.

"Great work yesterday," Eva says and hands me a Trenta-size Starbucks cup. The smell tells me it's dark roast with probably a couple of shots of espresso—my favorite. "Can't say the same for the guy following you," she adds. I take my seat at the conference table, eager to hear their assessment of smoker man. I'm also eager to not be alone with the unknown anymore.

"That was absolutely the worst display of surveillance I've ever seen," Denise says. "It was like he was daring you to notice him."

"That's exactly what he was doing," Neal says as he and Audrey walk in. They both look pressed and ready for the day, but exhausted. How late did everyone stay up last night going over the surveillance footage? Neal shuts the door behind him, letting us know that the meeting has begun.

"Though it may have appeared that the Russian following Kate yesterday was sloppy, I assure you that every move SVR makes is calculated," Audrey says. "Kate was tested yesterday, and she passed. All of you did a great job." Pride wells up in my chest as my team nods in thanks.

"The man following Kate yesterday doesn't match any of the known Russian operatives," Neal says. "My guess is that the Russians are being extra careful with this operation and have all new people working on it. They have a lot invested in Brittany and whoever else is out there, so this caution makes sense."

"But why make him so obvious? He did nothing to blend in. He stood and smoked like a European. And he was practically on my head," I say. "The way he was acting seemed more than a test. It felt like a statement."

"Y'all, I think the Russians are being cocky. They believe they've got a CIA officer in their pocket and it's gone to their head," Gina says.

"I'm much more inclined to think the Russians are arrogant rather than clueless. They have little, if any, ethics when it comes to espionage. They're not going to make it easy for you, Kate," Audrey says.

"I agree. The guy wasn't just annoying, he was creepy. I couldn't wait to get away from him," I say.

"Most likely, he'll be the one following you from now on. I don't think you should go running by yourself, even if it's a change in your routine," John says. "I know you can handle yourself, but to the Russians, you are now highly motivated to keep quiet. They could take advantage of that." He's right. As much as I hate to concede one more thing, I don't want to get caught alone with smoker man on a running trail, no matter how out of shape he is.

"I agree. I'll be sure and mention to Brittany that I pulled a muscle," I say.

We spend a good portion of the day going over the photos and drone footage. Smoker man never spoke to anyone or used his phone, so there was no opportunity to read his lips. I didn't recognize Denise anywhere and wondered if the team had purposely edited her out so they could use the same disguise another time. I didn't take the time to ask. It's much more important to find anything that can give us a lead with the Russians.

I get my first full look at smoker man's face, and the tingle of adrenalin lifts the skin on the back of my neck. *Be careful with this one*, says the voice in my head. I plan to do exactly that.

As we're wrapping up, Audrey asks a question I know is coming. "When do you feel it would be right to give Brittany the next feed material?"

"Brittany takes the baby on regular evening walks, but I never know if Guy's going to come along. And it feels too familiar of a setting for a conversation, so close to so many neighbors. And there's not as much masking noise as I'd like. I think she needs to give me a safer way to hand over the thumb drive. Or either set up a dead drop location," I say.

A dead drop is a method of tradecraft used to exchange information between two spies, usually an agent and their case officer. Often, it's used to protect an agent's identity, allowing one agent to leave information, for example, taped under a park bench to be picked up later by the case officer, the two having never met in person. If one is caught, they can't identify the other.

During the Cold War, agents were very creative in their efforts to keep anyone or anything from intercepting a dead drop. Information, usually film cartridges, were left in strategically positioned garbage no one would want to touch. Agents went as far as to soak dead rats in Tabasco sauce to keep other animals, let alone people, from taking the carcass. I wouldn't need to resort to rats, but I don't like the idea of leaving a thumb drive full of classified intelligence taped under a park bench.

"I'd feel better about you handing the feed material directly to Brittany, but I'll leave that up to you. Trust your gut. You'll know when it's right," Audrey says. I offer a quick prayer that I'll know when to make the next exchange.

I leave headquarters at five, exhausted and ready for a good night's sleep. Normally, I'd immediately change my clothes and go for a run to earn some ice cream later. But not tonight. I could run on my treadmill—something I hate even more than running on a trail—but, again, I have to assume someone is watching me. If I'm going to tell Brittany I've pulled a muscle and can't run, then I need to back up that lie.

When I pull into my driveway, I notice a pink envelope stuck in my front door. I know it's common for close neighbors to leave cards or invitations on doors rather than mail them. It's just not common for me because I don't know anyone well enough to warrant it, except Brittany.

I park my Tahoe and go directly to the front door. The envelope is the size of a thank you card and has my name on the front. I quickly go inside—no reason to hang out on the front porch and let the smoker man who followed me home watch me open the card.

On the outside of the card are the words "Thank you!" in pink script. On the inside is written
Dear Kate,

Words can't express our gratitude for the role you played in bringing our precious Kate into the world. We will be forever grateful!

We're also so thankful for the wonderful gifts and delicious dinner. The blanket, especially, is perfect for this time of year. I wrap Kate in it when we go to Kensington Heights Park every afternoon at two-thirty.

Thank you, again. Your friendship is one of the most important relationships in my life right now,

Brittany

Well, there's my sign.

Chapter Seventeen

Kensington Heights Park is a quick ten-minute drive from my neighborhood. It's a small park but has a nice playground with plenty of equipment for children to play on. John and I have taken Livvy there a few times, and she loved it.

The park is surrounded by oak and sycamore trees and lined with benches—the perfect place for moms to visit while their children play. There's no parking lot but plenty of street parking that's filling up quickly. Two-thirty is when schools let out and when the park fills up with moms and children. I see why Brittany chose this noisy time. I pull into a spot two cars down from Brittany's gray minivan.

I never thought about it until now, but it's odd that Brittany owns a minivan before she had children. Usually, that purchase, or vehicle concession, comes after a couple is outnumbered by their children. Is this Brittany trying a little too hard to look like the American mom?

The day is pleasant and sunny, with just enough breeze to keep the humidity comfortable. It's a perfect day for a visit to the park or, in my case, to hand over valuable secrets to the Russians. I wonder how many Americans would be shocked at the amount of espionage that takes place in everyday locations. I'm sure there are James Bond moments for every spy. I've had a few, some recently in Dubai. But the majority are just like what's about to happen—a thumb drive passing from one person to another while moms talk of effortless slow cooker recipes and summer day camps.

As I walk down the sidewalk toward the shrill of children's laughter and the metal squeak of swings in use, my hand instinctively checks my jean pocket for the white thumb drive Audrey slid across the table to me a week ago. It's there, of course. I've checked many times on the drive here. I'm wondering if I have OCD. Perhaps all spies do, eventually.

This batch of feed material is classified information regarding a new surveillance drone used by American operatives not only in Russia, but throughout the Middle East as well. This new drone has a broader, higher visual range with a much clearer picture. You don't know it's up there watching you, but it can capture a clear shot of a document you're holding.

This information was reclassified to appear more desirable for this exchange—a little trick the CIA has used successfully in other double agent operations. It's still risky but allows us to give up believable top secret intel that really isn't that top secret and doesn't cause as much damage. With what's on this thumb drive, the Russians will be on equal footing with American drone surveillance, or at least they'll think they are.

Although a drone doesn't feel as risky as a safe house that's protecting American operatives, I still experience the same nauseousness that was there with the last exchange. I put these emotions behind my mental curtain and push forward the revenge-seeking daughter of a spy. I'm going to do some more damage to the world of espionage that took my father from me.

Brittany has chosen a bench on the walking path a short distance from the playground. The sound of children playing and adults talking will still provide us with some sound masking, but not the curious eyes and interruptions that a bench right on the edge of the playground area might afford. She sits in the center of the bench, relaxed, with her legs crossed and arms draped across the back of the bench. This is a calculated move. If she were to sit on the end of the bench, it may invite another mom to join her and strike up a conversation that could be difficult to break off when I join them. I would have done the same thing. Social abruptness might often be interpreted as rudeness and would be remembered. Spies never want to be remembered.

Baby Kate is in her stroller with the shade pulled forward to protect her from the sunshine, but most likely to give the appearance that she's napping and discourage a passerby from admiring her. I'm happy to see that she really is napping.

"I love this park and it's so close," I say as I sit down just outside of Brittany's arm's reach. She smiles, folds her arms, and turns toward me. I hold my phone where she can see it and turn it off, then slide it in my back pocket.

Brittany's wearing black yoga pants and a long T-shirt. Her hair is pulled into a bun on the top of her head. She has no makeup on and the dark circles under her eyes are pronounced. Has she been up at night caring for baby Kate or secretly stealing Pentagon information from her husband and sending it to her contact here? Who are they and how is she doing it? I quickly quench the fire these questions ignite inside me.

"I know you do. You and John brought Livvy here a few times, am I correct?" she asks. Adrenalin ignites my face and ears. My jaw instantly clenches to stop it. How did she know that John and I have brought Livvy here? Those visits were months ago. How much does she know about me?

I try to calm the shock of her question, but she sees its effect on my face and slowly smiles. Brittany is reminding me she's in charge, that the Russian SVR is all knowing and all seeing, that they can get to anyone, anytime . . . even John and Livvy.

I want to lash out at Brittany, to threaten her and those she loves just like she did me. But who does she love? My reaction is instinctive and protective—we do anything to protect those we love. But, again, who does Brittany love? Just the thought of Brittany touching Livvy elicits a list of ways I could hurt Brittany—physical pain I'm sure she's been well trained to endure. Here she sits, though, with her newborn daughter who is nothing more to her than a means to an end. And here I sit with the flesh of my heart on fire with fear that those I love will be harmed. I'm sure the only fear Brittany has is the failure of her operation.

Your relationships will save you, says the voice in my head, reminding me of Audrey's council. *They are your strength.*

"Livvy does love it. Maybe, someday Kate will, too," I say. If baby Kate can play at this park someday, it may or may not be with her mom. Brittany is controlled by Russia; she could be here or in another part of the world. The possibility of not watching her daughter grow up probably means nothing to Brittany, but it would to me, so I said it. I want to remind her I have real, meaningful relationships in my life, and I don't view them as a weakness like she does.

Brittany's eyebrows come together and her nose twists as if she smells something offensive.

"Really? I doubt it. You Americans and your silly fantasies. I need to get home and start dinner," she says. She holds her hand out to me and purses her lips impatiently.

I want to grab baby Kate and run away from this heartless woman, but I go to get the thumb drive from my back pocket. My hand doesn't make it, though. My lungs burn with the sudden invasion of the sickening, acrid smoke I've logged into my memory. I gasp and cough to clear my lungs, my hand flying to my mouth to help.

About ten feet away, standing under a large oak tree, is smoker man. The breeze had brought a huge puff of smoke directly to my face and I unknowingly inhaled it.

"Guess those lungs of yours aren't what they used to be, are they?" Brittany says with a malicious grin. "A weakness like that would get me fired. But I guess your employers have lower standards."

I swallow the urge to cough and gain some control. My eyes are watering, but I can see the smile on smoker man's face as he exhales another cloud of toxic smoke.

"Here," I say with a raspy voice and hand Brittany the thumb drive. Baby Kate stirs awake, probably from my loud coughing. If Brittany notices, she doesn't show it.

"Don't mind Edgar over there. He's just doing his job, but you already know that," Brittany says. His laugh bounces through the air along with more smoke. She stands and unlocks the wheels of the stroller. "I'll be in touch. If this is as good as the last one, there'll be a payment in your account. Twenty grand." She walks off with the now crying baby Kate and a smug, smoking Edgar.

Despite all I just went through, headquarters just heard through the microphone on my earring that smoker man has a name. I imagine with great delight the smile on Gina's face.

I get up and walk in the opposite direction than I came. I'll take the long way around the playground area and back to my Tahoe to enjoy some fresh air. I never got around to showing Brittany my pretend pulled muscle, but I don't care. If she asks me why I'm suddenly not going on my daily runs, I'll tell her I don't want to with Edgar smoking in my face. And then she can have a good laugh, which I'm sure she'll enjoy.

Chapter Eighteen

I spent another sleepless night of not knowing—the outcome of the drone intelligence and who Edgar is. When I stand in the doorway of the conference room, I can tell the team and John have been hard at work for hours. Gina has a can of Red Bull next to her laptop, but by the way she's typing, I can tell it's not her first, or her fourth. Her blonde hair is limp and coming out of its ponytail, and her eye makeup has the faded, smudged look that tells me it was applied yesterday and not this morning. When she sees me, she not only stops typing, but also closes her laptop.

"Hey, honey. How are ya this morning?" she asks. If calling me honey wasn't sign enough that something was wrong, then closing her laptop is. Denise, Eva, and John, all too busy to notice me in the doorway, stop what they're working on and look up at me. Fear grips my stomach and twists.

"What? What is it?" I ask. I want to know right now what's going on. I've had it with the not knowing.

"Have a seat," John says and pulls a chair out for me. I hold his eyes for a second and all I see is exhaustion and worry. I slowly sit down and Denise scoots a Starbucks cup towards me, but I hold my hand up to refuse it. Coffee, or anything else, wouldn't stay down right now.

Nobody opens their laptop or reaches for papers or notes, which tells me that what they're about to tell me they know by heart—they've been absorbing this information all night.

"We found out who Edgar is," John says. The pause of silence that follows this announcement speaks volumes to me—if my team is hesitant to tell me, it's bad.

"And . . ." I say. Eva exhales and folds her arms.

"Edgar is the assassin Lot," Eva says. Long, hot fingers of fear slide across my head and then squeeze. I close my eyes and clench my jaw to withstand the pain. I take a deep inhale through my nose and open my eyes. "You probably already know this, but he's Romanian by birth but was recruited by the KGB at a young age, possibly in his twenties. Of course, when the SVR was organized, they kept him as a contract killer," Eva adds, and I nod.

Lot never goes by his real name, and I doubt Edgar is it. Lot is an acronym of sorts. It stands for Leave Zero Trace. In every case that Lot's been employed—many times over his notorious career—there has never been a trace of evidence left. And no one ever found a body. Not one.

My ears are ringing and my mouth is dry, but I don't dare try to swallow anything. Yes, I've heard of Lot. Everyone in intelligence has. And the biblical story of Lot's wife turning into salt is not lost on me.

"Lot. The famous assassin who makes people disappear. Lot, who has lived into his sixties, which is almost unheard of in his line of work. He's the dude who followed me to the cleaners?" I ask. I say this last part a little too loudly and wave my hands in apology.

"That's the one," John says quietly. I swallow and nod, and then I take a few deep breaths.

"Why?" I ask. There's more silence, but along with it is the sense that everyone is planning their best guess—what they all have been working on for hours.

"It seems like overkill," Gina says. We all wince at her choice of words, but she seems to not notice. "I did some digging around on the dark web and found Mr. Lot's asking price. Mother Russia is paying a ton of money to have him run errands with y'all. And I don't know if this helps or not, but I did uncover his real name. It's Igorash Rotari. Fits, huh?" We all nod in silence. Images of cartoon Gothic villains flash across my mind. Of course his real name is Igor.

"If nothing else, it shows us just how crucial Brittany's cover is to Russia," Denise says. "Whatever she and her people are working on, they really don't want you messing up, so they're covering all their bases. If you become a liability to Brittany, they'll have you disappear. It will draw some attention, but no one will find anything, or you." I figured Lot's services didn't come cheap, but I hadn't yet thought through all that hiring him to watch me entails.

"So, as Russia sees it, if I expose Brittany and confess to the CIA, I'm put away for life as a traitor, along with Brittany. But the rest of Brittany's group goes dark and we never find them. If Brittany's apprehended, she'll never talk and she or Lot will destroy all the evidence that would lead us to anyone. If I keep feeding information to Brittany and keep my mouth shut, Russia is happy and I get my revenge. But—and this is a big one—I've seen Lot's face and heard his voice. He will not let me live no matter how this plays out for Russia," I say.

Assassins, especially the caliber of Lot, live in the dark. They have no relationships. Their identity is sacred and never exposed—it's how they stay alive. They certainly don't follow CIA operatives to Safeway and the cleaners unless a great deal is on the line. Unless, of course, they are assured it will all work out to their advantage. They are confident they can kill whoever sees them, just like any other job. One thing is certain, though, in the eyes of Russia: I was dead the minute I heard Brittany scream in her native tongue.

"We're gonna get you out of this mess. We're gonna get what information we need and we're gonna get you out," Gina says.

"How? Brittany hates America and all Americans. She will not allow me to get close enough to confide in me who she's working with. I'll have to steal it somehow," I say. After our visit at the park, Brittany probably is looking forward to the day that she can give Lot the nod to take me out. There won't be any cozy lunches where she lets her guard down.

"You're right. You'll have to steal it. And I'm gonna make that easy and painless. I'm sure Brittany's working off her phone—it has the same capacity as a computer and is much easier to destroy if she needs to. My tech guys and I are fixin' up an app that'll download whatever's on Brittany's phone and she'll never know it. You'll just have to be within a few feet of her phone with yours. It will take a few days, though. I'm sure her phone is heavily encrypted, so it'll take some fancy footwork on our part," Gina says. Relief warms through my body and the long fingers of fear loosen their grip on my head. Could it really be that easy?

"That would be great," I say and release a long exhale.

"In the meantime, you just keep giving Brittany the feed material and keep a safe distance from Lot. The park is a great place to make the transfer," John says. "Maxwell is arranging under cover special agents to watch you. Brittany and Lot won't know they're there." I nod as more relief flows through my nervous system.

If this were a normal scenario where it's just me against an enemy, I would openly protect myself. But with Brittany, if I do anything to fight against her or her people, I expose myself as a double agent and the lives of all those I love are in danger, not to mention countless lives in the intelligence community. I feel helpless and I hate it.

"There's one more thing," John says. "I think it's time we reach out for some additional help. Neal and Audrey agree."

"Okay. What kind of help?" I ask. Do we need even more FBI special agents?

"It's time we contact your dad."

Chapter Nineteen

Manny Russo owns and runs Manny's Italian Restaurant. He's huge, with a meaty face and fingers the size of large sausages, but he can glide through the tables of his small restaurant like a figure skater. Manny is a gifted cook and has some of the best Italian recipes in the DC area. He is also the only way I can contact my father.

Manny isn't in intelligence. He's just a trusted friend to my father. And because of that trust, Manny knows more about my father than I do. Though frustrating, the two men are going to keep it that way for my protection. If I need my father, though, Manny can reach him.

Manny may not be a spy, but he understands the world of espionage. A man that has kept the true identity of James McLean a secret for so long would have to. Manny and my father follow strict protocols with up-to-date technology to detect bugs and surveillance. But they also use old-school tradecraft, as well. For years, my father sent notes to my mother using Morse code, and that's how I communicate with him now—dots and lines on the back of a Manny's Restaurant order ticket. To most people, it would look like someone's attempt to pass the time with a Sudoku game.

Although Manny has been careful over the years, I still worry about coming here for dinner with John this evening. Lot pulled out behind us as we left my house in John's truck. We timed our visit to Manny's between the lunch and dinner crowds hoping to have a private word with Manny, but no matter how well we planned, our night out at Manny's will include Lot.

There are no cars parked in front of Manny's and John pulls into a space directly in front. I don't turn around to see where Lot parks, but I know he's back there somewhere. Keeping his head facing forward, John looks in the rearview mirror.

"He parked at the end of the block on the same side of the street," John says. "But I don't think he'll come in because he can't smoke in Manny's." I give him a quick nod of agreement.

"I just wonder how close he'll come. Will he stand in front of the window trying to read our lips?" I ask.

"Well, there's only one way to find out. But if he does, I'll act as if I'm going to the restroom and talk to Manny in the kitchen," John says. Manny's just has one restroom and it's off of the kitchen, so this situation gives us the perfect cover. I hope it doesn't come to this, though. I'd like to tell Manny to his face what's going on—talking to Manny is the closest thing I have to talking to my father.

The cherry tree in the front of Manny's has already bloomed and leafed out. It's a nonfruiting tree, so there are no bright-red clusters of cherries. Its oblong, bright-green leaves will remain until fall. Coming to Manny's throughout my childhood has caused me to be acutely aware of the blooming cycle of cherry trees. When

THE PITCH

I'd see cherry blossoms on trees in our neighborhood, I'd beg my mom to go to Manny's so we could sit under the "flower tree."

Memories of Manny's and pink cherry blossoms flash through my mind as John and I walk under the leaf-filled branches. My lips tighten at the thought that these beautiful leaves will be smothered with an assassin's cigarette smoke for the next few hours. Like everything else since I became a double agent, this part of my life is invaded.

The bell on the door jingles and Manny glides through empty tables and chairs to greet us with a sweaty, flour-covered hug. It's all normal. It's all the same as every time we've come for spaghetti and lasagna—it has to be. But it's not. My chest tightens as I see Lot's profile walk past the front window.

Manny chats and smiles and seats us in our usual booth toward the back of the empty restaurant. This time, though, I sit with my back to the entrance. John and I have been trained to always keep entrances and exits in our line of sight. To see who's coming and going gives you an advantage in any situation.

Over the years, this bit of tradecraft has not just been useful, but has also become a significant source of security. For most spies, it's extremely uncomfortable to sit with your back to the entrance, which is why John always allows me to sit in the booth's side that gives me the view of the front door. Not today, though. It would be too easy for Lot to see what I'm saying.

Manny knows why John usually sits where he sits and picks up on this change immediately. He looks at John, then me, then back at John, then out the front window at Lot, who is leaning against the cherry tree, smoking. Manny turns slightly so Lot can't see his face.

"You two going to tell me what's going on or what?" he asks. His eyes keep moving between John and me, and he folds his large arms over his barrel chest.

John knocks a menu off the table, and while leaning down to get it, says, "I'll go to the restroom in a minute and tell you. We need your help." Manny drops his arms and clenches both his large hands into fists. His eyes narrow on me until all I see are his bushy eyebrows.

"Does it have to do with that guy out there?" he asks us.

"Yes," I whisper. Manny thinks for a minute and his fleshy lips draw into a thin line.

"Water and bread," he says and thumps the table twice with his large finger. He shoves two chairs out of place as he awkwardly makes his way back to the kitchen.

"Manny can't be on Lot's radar," I say.

"He won't be. We're just having an early dinner at our favorite restaurant. Lot hasn't looked in the window once, and I doubt he could read lips this far away," John says.

Manny comes out of the kitchen with two glasses of water and a large loaf of fresh-baked bread on a tray. As usual, there's no knife. In Manny's world, bread is to be torn, not sliced.

"You want the usual?" Manny asks.

"That would be great," I answer and try to give a normal smile. Manny's glare bores a hole in my head. He looks at John, then out the front window, then back at me.

"The usual, then," Manny says, thumps the table twice, and bumps chairs all the way back into the kitchen.

THE PITCH

I'm not hungry, but I tear off a piece of bread and eat it. So does John. This is what we always do when we go out to dinner.

We hear a steady increase of clashing dishes in the kitchen and give each other a nod—it's time for John to "use the restroom."

"I'll be back in a few minutes," John says. He slides the chairs Manny displaced back to where they belong and then quietly goes through the kitchen door. The sounds from the kitchen immediately stop, and I offer a silent prayer that Manny will understand. Several minutes pass with just the low hum of the air conditioner. I eat two more bites of bread and do my best to appear relaxed, but I can't stop my mind from wondering. Just how much does Manny know about the world of espionage? Can he stay safe? I have to trust my father and Manny's friendship, but there are so many things I don't know.

My heart jumps against my chest as the bell on the door jingles. Is Lot actually coming in to check on me? Did he see John go back into the kitchen with Manny? I exhale quietly when I hear the relaxed exchange between a man and a woman. I look back toward the door as a couple comes in and waits to be seated. The faint scent of Lot's cigarette smoke stings my nose and I sneeze. Once again, I'm amazed at how pervasive and far-reaching smoke can be.

"Sit wherever you like," Manny tells the couple. He's holding two plates, one heaped with spaghetti and the other lasagna—always three times what we can eat. John sits down as Manny sets the plates on our table. "I'll leave this here now," Manny says and slides the ticket toward me. I watch as he lithely maneuvers past three tables to greet the couple who sat down at a table next to the front window. I look far enough up to see Lot's feet. He's still leaning against the tree. A cigarette butt lands next to his foot and he smashes it into the sidewalk.

"It'll be okay," John says quietly. I slowly turn the ticket over to find a series of dots and lines—Morse code written by Manny. This time, though, the message is from Manny and not my father.

"Your dad will know by tonight. Don't worry. He and I know what to do."

Relief slackens my jaws and drops my shoulders. I take in a deep, calm breath of air. In a few brief hours, my father will know that I'm a double agent with a notorious, skilled assassin watching my every move. He knows I've never had a cover like this and he'll know how I feel—isolated, frightened, and determined to succeed. He and Manny will take measures to help and protect me. What these measures are, I don't know. They wouldn't tell me if I asked them. *Your relationships will save you*, says the voice in my head. *Trust in the Lord and have peace.*

I swirl spaghetti around my fork and then put the sauce-covered noodles in my mouth like I do every time I'm at Manny's. This evening can't be any different. Everything has to be the same.

Chapter Twenty

Livvy greets me at the door and immediately begins telling me about her end-of-the-year party at preschool earlier today. I give her a quick hug and she smells of construction paper and icing.

"We made mailboxes last week, like we did at Valentine's Day but without the hearts," Livvy says. I nod, encouraging her to keep telling me about it. She leads me by the hand to the living room. Rose is in the kitchen making what looks like a green salad. She gives me a knowing smile as Livvy chatters on.

"Dinner will be ready soon," Rose says quickly. Livvy tugs at my hand, a signal to sit on the floor and look at her mailbox from school.

"We gave each other drawings of what we'll be doing this summer," Livvy says. On the rug is a box covered with crayon-drawn flowers I recognize as Livvy's. Surrounding the box are several drawings that I can tell were drawn by other children.

"You did such a good job with your mailbox," I tell Livvy. She beams and picks it up to show me the slot on top and how the folded drawings can slide through.

"Aiden is going to California to go to Disneyland with his mean grandmother," Livvy says and hands me a drawing of what appears to be an elderly woman with mouse ears. She is clearly angry and appears to be pointing at several small children. I roll my lips inward to keep from laughing and then glance over at Rose. With pursed lips and raised eyebrows, she continues chopping vegetables.

Livvy keeps handing me drawings and telling me of the summer adventures of her classmates. Mia will go to the beach with her cousins. Chloe will take a train to New York City to see the Statue of Liberty. Mateo will go to a family reunion in Colorado.

"Sophia is going on a big boat to islands where there are fancy fish," Livvy says. These trips she has described sound fun, yet there hasn't been a note of jealousy in her voice. I know John has worked with her on expressing happiness for others and taking her turn—we all get our chance to open birthday presents. But I know she's old enough to experience envy.

"What did you draw?" I ask her. John and I have planned a few trips with her for summer break—to Walt Disney World Resort in Florida and a weekend stay at a water park here in Maryland. I assumed she would draw one of these.

"I drew you and me and dad and grandma eating in the garden," she says matter-of-factly. My heart pushes against my chest and I swallow to keep my eyes dry. Of all the happy places she'll go this summer, it's at home with her family that tops the list. I look over Livvy's head to Rose, who is smiling at us. She gives me a wink, then turns to get what smells like baking bread out of the oven.

The last twenty minutes have been such a diversion that I haven't thought about anything but mean, mouse-eared grandmas and fancy fish until John comes in. For a second, his jaw is clenched and his eyes are narrowed—he saw Lot parked down the street where he was when I walked in earlier. At the first glimpse of his daughter and me, the frustration leaves his face. He pulls his tie through his collar and tosses it on the sofa, then unbuttons the top button of his white dress shirt. Though I've seen him do this many times, he's so handsome I can't not watch him. He catches my eyes, then smothers my face with kisses—a look I've seen many times but still takes my breath.

Livvy launches herself onto her father as if she hasn't seen him for weeks—a sight I'll never tire seeing. He rolls onto the floor next to me and proceeds to tickle Livvy until the house fills with her trilling laughter. How can so much evil be sitting in a car just down the road?

Livvy gives another rendition of the end-of-the year party, which produces sufficient exclamations from her father. Watching John stifle his laughter when shown the drawing of the mouse-eared mean grandmother made me forget Lot and Brittany and Russia for a few seconds.

We eat leftovers from Manny's with fresh-baked French bread and salad. The evening is mild so we eat in the garden—nothing fancy, but the garden is such an Eden this time of year that no one would miss tablecloths and china. Paper plates are just fine. The peach cobbler and homemade vanilla ice cream are delectable. John and I keep eating out of the pan as we talk.

I know John wants to tell me something privately when he whispers a few words to his mom, who immediately takes Livvy inside. The table has been cleared and the food put away, so I don't feel too guilty about leaving Rose with glasses and silverware.

The fountain has been running all evening, but John adjusts it to run faster and, therefore, creates more sound to mask our voices. We sit on the bench and then I turn toward John, expecting him to talk, but he doesn't. Instead, he pulls my face to his and kisses me. He doesn't stop with one, but keeps kissing me until we both pull away for air.

"I've wanted to do that since I walked in the house," he says through intakes of breath. I smile and rest my forehead against his.

"Is that why your mother is cleaning the kitchen by herself and your daughter is trying to watch us through the curtains?" I ask. We both look at the sliding glass door just as the curtains wave and a small hand disappears. John laughs but shakes his head.

"No. It's only part of the reason. I stayed a few minutes at work to get clearance on something I want to tell you," he says. My eyebrows come together. We both have the same security clearance at the CIA, so I can't imagine what this could be. And then hot pinpricks of adrenalin run across my body. Does this have to do with the time he worked deep cover with my father? This question must have shown on my face because John nods.

"There are some parts of your father's skill as a spy that may help you now," he says. The hunger to know anything about my father widens my eyes. I motion him with my hand to keep talking.

"I can't tell you where we were, but it's really not important. I was in trouble. My cover had been blown, my comms was gone, and I needed extraction. I was panicking and not thinking straight. I let myself get trapped in an alleyway with no way to change my profile," he says.

"Who were after you?" I blurt out.

"I can't tell you that, either," he says. I roll my eyes but nod. I should be used to the proverbial air quotes that can be around the term "clearance" when used by the CIA, but sometimes it still frustrates me. Like right now.

"Out of nowhere, a rope drops in front of me. I look up and your father's face appears over the edge of the roof. 'Climb' he tells me and I do, the fastest I ever have in my life. Once I was on the roof, he had me stand in the center of the building's roof so I wouldn't be visible to those on the ground. He had all the pieces to help me change my profile, then I jumped into the back of a hay truck waiting on the other side of the building. I hid between the bales of hay until I was out of the city," John says.

This is a great story. I want to hear everything I can about my father, but I don't understand why John would get clearance for this particular extraction, and I tell him as much.

"My point is, your father was completely calm through all of that extraction. He was certain about every move he made. When I asked him about it later, he said he was just following his instinct that told him what to do. He said he knew beyond any doubt that I'd make it out." I know what John's talking about, what voice my father was listening to that gave him such confidence.

"When I listen to the voice in my head, it feels like that sometimes. Like I'm less Kate the person and more Kate the spy, going on faith."

"I know you do. I've seen it. Your father works the same way. He made a path for me where there wasn't one—where I couldn't imagine there being one. You can do the same," he says. I smile, understanding now why he shared the details of this extraction with me. He wants me to trust my instincts and showed me a pattern with my father.

"Thank you for telling me this," I say and give him a kiss. Out of the corner of my eye, I see the curtains move again and I break the kiss with a smile. "And now if you'll excuse me, I'll go read your daughter her bedtime stories I promised." I move to stand but he pulls be back down for one more long kiss.

Chapter Twenty-One

Since the last day of school was yesterday, the park is packed by two-thirty in the afternoon with happy children, free for the summer. The sound of laughter and swings and the crunch of gravel blur into one crush of noise as I turn onto the walking path where I met Brittany last time. In the distance, I see her sitting on a bench with a stroller next to her. Lot will be along soon. He followed me here. Gina can't make that app soon enough.

The white thumb drive I received from Audrey yesterday is in my pocket. This one contains more specs on surveillance drones. The Russians must have liked the last drone intel because it earned me twenty thousand dollars that was deposited in my offshore account. The idea of receiving money for American secrets makes my stomach turn, even if I know the damage was minimal. How do people *really* do this?

"I bet this isn't anything like spring in Russia," I say as I sit on the bench. "I've never been there." It's true. I haven't. My work has primarily been in the Middle East. But I'm sure Brittany knows all of this.

I set my phone between us and turn it off. Even though Gina is working night and day to create the app that will save me, I have to try to get something from Brittany. I want to catch her off guard and get her to say something about her life before she came to America. She turns towards me and slowly smiles.

Her hair hangs straight and looks as if she has spent some time on it. She wears a loose-fitting maxi dress with sandals. But the extra grooming doesn't hide the exhaustion that hangs in dark circles under her eyes.

"You Americans are so chatty. It's the one part of my cover I hate more than the rest," she says. I glance toward baby Kate asleep in the stroller. She looks like an angel wrapped in the white blanket I gave her. I guess she's a part of what Brittany hates too, just not as much as small talk.

Not for the first time I want to grab baby Kate and run. My nose tingles at a whiff of Lot's cigarette smoke, and I am reminded that everything I do and say is being scrutinized carefully by unseen Russian SVR agents. Can I be trusted? Am I a double? Will FBI agents swoop in from nowhere and arrest Brittany and Lot? My life hangs in the balance of these questions that I imagine Russia asks repeatedly. The slightest nuance could raise a red flag, even a glance toward a sleeping baby. I have to be careful. Like John told me last night, I must trust my instinct. There will be a time soon to rescue baby Kate.

"Thanks for the payment, but the revenge is sweeter," I say. I slide the thumb drive out of my pocket and hand it to her. "We've been working on this for a while. I'm sure your people will like it." Brittany takes the thumb drive from me and tosses it next to her sleeping child. Baby Kate twitches, then relaxes back to sleep. Without another word, Brittany stands and then pushes the stroller down the walking path. I say a silent prayer that this precious child will end up with her father and be safe. *She will*, says the voice in my head.

I exhale and stand. I'm eager to be away from Lot, who is smoking under the same tree as our last meeting. There was no intel gathered from this exchange. Nothing, except Brittany hates small talk and Lot is still watching my every move. I'll drive back to headquarters and see if they got anything I missed.

Gina is the first one in the conference room. She's seated at the table, typing like crazy on her laptop, but stops when she sees me.

"Y'all, I don't care if she's baby Kate's momma. The sooner that child is away from that horrible woman, the better," Gina says. Red Bull is hiding Gina's exhaustion, but I can see through it. Makeup and mega doses of caffeine can't hide the tired she's experiencing.

"I couldn't agree with you more. Brittany won't mistreat her, though. The last thing she'll do is blow her cover with her husband. I promise, Guy thinks Brittany's the best mother in the world." I can hardly say these words without choking.

John, Denise, and Eva come into the conference room where Gina and I are. Audrey and Maxwell are the last to join us. We're gathering to go over my meeting with Brittany an hour ago, and to make some sort of plan to move forward. We listen to the few words Brittany and I exchanged and I fill them in on the rest. There's not much to go on.

"My special agents followed you. Lot's keeping close. The fact that they have that sicko assassin following you is a sign that this is bigger than anyone thinks. I want Kate out of this. Now," says Maxwell. Everyone here knows that Maxwell blew a gasket when he found out Lot the assassin was Russia's choice for my shadow.

"I couldn't agree with you more. But we've got to try to get at least some of the people Brittany's working with. It's what our job is," Audrey says to Maxwell. He's started sweating and I can see the vein on his forehead pulsing from across the table. "Gina, what's your best guess for completion of the app?"

"We're close. Four or five days. We're trying to make it so all Kate has to do is have her phone a foot from Brittany's, but she may need to actually have the two phones touch, which, of course, could blow her cover," Gina says. If I have to touch Brittany's phone with mine, she would know immediately that I've compromised her. It wouldn't give me much of a chance to get away. Of course, Lot would be close by.

"It has to be twelve inches," Maxwell says. "Your phone was that close to Brittany's in the park. She would've never known you copied it until you were safely away." Everyone nods.

"Then that's what we'll do," Gina says. "I know you make sure Brittany watches you turn your phone off, but all it would take is a few seconds next to hers to copy what we need, like a five count before you turn yours off." I close my eyes for a second and nod. The idea of having the intel we need in five seconds and being done with this operation is a relief beyond words. John lays his hand on my forearm and gives it a squeeze.

"It won't be long now," he says.

"I've got two more thumb drives for you. This white one is another safe house in Moscow. We're prepared like the first one, so hopefully no one will be compromised," Audrey says. "This pink thumb drive is the identity of an American officer. His cover is at the embassy, so he'll have diplomatic immunity. But his career in intelligence would be over. This officer will be a big win for the Russians. If you have to use this, you can tell Brittany you've been working on this from the beginning. It would make sense for this type of intel to take longer to acquire. We have extraction ready for him at a moment's notice. It would be good, though, if we didn't have to use it."

"Y'all will have to sacrifice that safe house, but I'm gonna do everything in my power to save that officer," Gina says.

"In the meantime, I'll keep trying to get something from Brittany, but I don't think she's going to give us anything," I say.

"She's not," Denise says. "I think our best bet is for Lot to tire of this job that is clearly beneath him and slip up." Audrey and John both nod.

"Well, I've got another bunch of errands to run tomorrow. We're all set, right?" I ask.

"I'll be out there in my disguise," Denise says.

"And the drones will be up and flying," Eva says.

"My agents will be ghosts. He'll never see them," Maxwell says. "But I don't want you taking any risks. This is a waiting game for you. Am I clear?" I nod, but his vein is still dancing on his forehead.

"It'll be just another afternoon of errands. Lot will be bored out of his mind," I say.

Chapter Twenty-Two

Something's wrong. I sit up in bed. The back of my neck is wet with sweat. My heart rate increases as my eyes move from one wall to the next in my bedroom. A faint blue light outlines the curtains on my window. It's early. A glance at my clock confirms it—5:45.

Something's wrong, repeats the voice in my head. I don't need her to repeat it. I can feel that something is terribly wrong. The space around me is suspicious, as if it's waiting for the truth, but not sure it will get it. Until it does, it surrounds me with its questions.

I get up and walk from room to room. This warning has nothing to do with the state of my home, but I do this walk-through anyway. All is as it should be. Everything is where I left it in my entryway—keys and sunglasses on the glass table, my black go bag on the floor under the table.

My fingers twitch with a sudden urge to grab the go bag and run—my body responding to years of training. In minutes, I could look like a completely different person on a bus going out of the city. *Not yet*, says the voice, and she's right. My disappearance could cost others their lives, at the very least their careers in intelligence. I would never do that to my team and never leave John without him knowing. But in my heart, I know as a double agent it could come to this.

I walk from room to room and the feeling moves with me. There's something wrong. Really wrong. This space around me can only keep what's wrong at bay for so long and then, when the truth comes, this space will dissipate like morning fog under the bright light of the sun. Until then, I'll keep wading through this murky space of response without a reason, this unknown. So much of being a double agent is staying calm while living with the unknown. I don't like it. How does my father do it? How did John do it? No wonder John felt at times like he was losing it.

I peek through my front blinds and see that nothing is unusual at Brittany and Guy's house. That's not much of an assurance, though. Things are never what they seem behind the walls of that lovely suburban home.

My mind works through yesterday afternoon—my errand running with Lot. It was a long afternoon and Lot was with me the whole time—at the bank, the cleaners, the car wash. He stood and smoked outside the nail salon as I got a pedicure, whiffs of his obnoxious cigarette smoke coming in with each person who entered and left. By the time I hit Safeway, I was so tired of his eyes on me I spent an extra fifty dollars on items I didn't need to warrant the extra time I spent in the store. Of course, he wouldn't come into the store because he couldn't smoke.

I could have run. I could have left out the back door of the store. I could have used my quick-change disguise I carry in my purse and disappeared. In a normal surveillance situation where I would have been trying to lose whomever was following me, this is exactly what I would have done. But playing the cat-and-mouse game of a double agent operation, I have to pretend as if Lot isn't there. I can't look back, let alone disappear out the back door.

Though exhausting, the afternoon produced no red flags or valuable intel. Lot never used his phone, giving us a chance to catch a phone number or a name on the drone footage. Lot spoke to no one, though from the footage, several people gave him questioning looks and would probably remember the strange man smoking outside the nail salon. Once again, he appeared as a sloppy agent performing unprofessional surveillance. But he's really one of the best assassins in the world, one who could make anybody who got in his way, or even annoyed him, disappear forever.

The switch on my coffee machine makes a louder-than-normal click and a brief surge of adrenalin prickles my face. I inhale and exhale slowly to clear away this chemical my body produces to warn me of danger and activate the instinct to flee or fight. I can do neither right now. I must live in this moment of uncertainty, mucking through this awful space, pretending it's all normal until I can find out the truth.

Being a double agent has been referred to as the Navy SEALs of espionage and I get that now, though this is hardly an equal comparison—I've seen some of the superhuman feats SEALs have done and an afternoon shopping with Lot hardly compares. But the emotional control of hiding my life behind a curtain has been incredibly taxing, much like what former SEALs have told me they've experienced on missions.

The Isaiah scripture comes to my mind and the promise of perfect peace if I trust the Lord. I lean against the kitchen counter and close my eyes. Can I really have peace amid so much uncertainty and such a complex web of lies?

The coffee machine fills my mug with the dark, warm liquid. I don't jump at the sound, but I keep my eyes closed and allow it to wash over me. Thoughts of John's fountain in Rose's garden calms me even more—the safety I feel sitting next to John in a space where we can speak freely. We're not spies next to the fountain, just John and Kate with fears and doubts that we shoulder together. *Your relationships will save you*, says the voice. *You need to talk to John.*

The coffee machine clicks off and I open my eyes. My mug is full. I take it out of the machine and go to get ready. I can be at headquarters in less than an hour.

Chapter Twenty-Three

John takes one look at my eyes, comes into my office, and shuts the door behind him. He keeps his eyes on my face as he sits across the desk from me.

"You know that voice in my head, the one I trust, the one that reminds you of my father, the one that's never wrong?" I ask.

"Yes," John says, urging me to continue.

"It woke me up this morning, telling me something is wrong. I didn't need to hear the words, though. I felt it. I still feel it." John holds my eyes for three long beats. He is my safe place and his eyes always steady me as they are right now. He won't question me. He knows the feeling I'm talking about. I can tell by his eyes he's felt this "something's wrong" feeling before.

"Did everything look normal at the Halls'?" he asks. I shrug.

"From the outside," I say. He nods because he knows that normal on the outside doesn't mean much. "But Lot didn't follow me to work this morning. I haven't seen him. He's always behind me." John sits stone-still except for the quick clenching and unclenching of his jaw.

"What does your gut tell you?" he asks. He folds his arms and exhales, bracing for my answer.

"It feels like Brittany knows I'm a double. That somehow, she found out. But how? We've been so careful."

"Let's call a meeting with everyone. But we need to tell Audrey this right now," he says.

"This is one time I really hope my instinct is wrong," I say.

"You're too much like your father for that to happen," he says. I close my eyes for a second but open them at the sound of John's chair sliding. He comes to my side of the desk and pulls me up and into a hug.

Though my office door is closed, someone could still tap a few times and enter. But right now I don't care, and clearly John doesn't either. I'm frightened and I need his strength. His arms pull me a little closer and I hear the steady rhythm of his heart beat. He brushes my ear with a kiss and then rests his chin on my head.

"We'll work this out, you and I. It will all work out, I promise," he says. We both know it could all go horribly wrong really fast, but I let him assure me. I let his words sink into my heart and give me faith. After a moment, I pull away and hold his eyes. They're worried but not sagging with sadness like I've seen so many times.

"I love you. We will. We'll work this out," I say. He cradles my face in his hands and tenderly kisses me, then whispers against my lips that he loves me, too. I'm not alone in this awful space that I woke up in.

He kisses me once more, then tells me he'll be right back with Audrey and that he'll also send the word out for a meeting in an hour. I nod and watch him leave and close the door behind him. I walk to the window and lift the blinds to a radiantly sunny day. There should be no reason for Brittany to not be at the park this afternoon. I could meet her there and give her the thumb drive with the safe house information. If I keep to the time frame I've set, it would be feasible for me to have produced this intel for her by now. I could know by this afternoon why I feel the way I do.

A light tap sounds at the door and John and Audrey enter. John's eyes are still worried, but for the first time, I see Audrey visibly concerned—her eyes are drawn wide and immediately begin assessing me. John pulls a chair over for Audrey and we all sit. Audrey sits upright with her arms folded, her right leg bouncing slightly. I hear the fabric of her pants brushing against the front of my desk.

"Tell me everything. Leave nothing out," she says. I know I'm not the only double agent operation she has running right now, but her nervousness would make me believe otherwise.

I explain to her how my instinct works as a voice in my head—like my own voice, but not. It guides me and is always right. And then I tell her how I woke up to the voice telling me that something was wrong . . . and I have an overwhelming sense that, once again, the voice is right.

We sit in silence for a minute, the lines between Audrey's eyebrows never relaxing once. Her eyes study my desk, but I imagine they are seeing timelines and scenarios, much like what I've done since I woke up.

"They're testing you. We all know that the vetting of an agent never ends—we're constantly assessing them for their truthfulness. Perhaps Brittany or Lot were spooked by something. If they suspected someone following you yesterday and ask you about it, you can always act frightened, as if the CIA is on to you. You have been producing a lot of intel for her. It would make sense that we are suspicious and put a tail on you. Keep to your regular schedule. Go to the park this afternoon with a thumb drive. That will tell us something," Audrey says.

"The main thing to remember is to put all your fear behind the curtain. Act normal," John says. "If Brittany questions you about anything, blame your fear of being considered a mole. She'll believe it. It has to be a real fear of hers, as well."

"Maxwell will want to put more special agents out there to watch you, and I'm going to let him," Audrey says. I nod, knowing there's not much we can do to stop him. Frankly, I want a crowd of ghosts around me when I walk into that park this afternoon. John looks at his phone and then stands.

"Everyone is gathered in the conference room. Let's go."

Chapter Twenty-Four

There's no gray Impala behind me as I drive to the park, nor is there one on the surrounding streets. I find an open space close to the walking trail where I usually meet Brittany and park. It's 2:20 p.m., the time I normally arrive.

The sky is a cloudless cornflower-blue and I feel the warmth of the sun through my T-shirt. The laughs and shouts from the children on the playground fill the air. A little girl swings higher and higher on a swing as her friend dares her to go even higher. Her long, blonde hair covers her face each time she swings backwards, and she tries to brush it aside without letting go of the chain. I stand and watch her for a minute, stalling. The little girl finally slows and puts her hair behind her ears, beaming at her friends.

I turn and force myself to look at the walking path. There's no woman sitting on the bench with a stroller next to her. As I get closer to the bench, the air is clear—there's no Lot standing under the tree smoking. I look in all directions, but there's no Brittany and I know she's not coming. But I sit and wait.

Wait an hour. They're watching, says the voice in my head. I know they're watching from somewhere. Perhaps Lot is exercising the surveillance skills we all know he must have. If he can find people that are impossible to find and make them disappear, then he can be invisible. But he'd have to stop smoking to do that. It's been my experience that it's the little things that can mess up even the most skilled bad guys, especially when it comes to the addictive habit of smoking. I take a few deep breaths, trying to detect even a hint of Lot's cigarette smoke, but there's none.

Is this a normal test that Russia puts all their agents through? I know that a good portion of their protocols are dramatically different from ours, but my gut tells me they wouldn't break contact with an agent unless something was wrong. And something *is* wrong.

I run through the different scenarios my team helped me come up with in the meeting—the CIA found where someone accessed the location of a safe house with no reason, the drone intel has been tampered with, files were copied without clearance. All these reasons would warrant an investigation and have counterintelligence assign an officer to follow me.

Audrey was right. Maxwell has put even more special agents on me. He was so upset in the meeting, I'm surprised I haven't seen him abandoning all protocols, standing on the other side of the park angrily watching me. What debt does he owe my father that can only be repaid by protecting me?

Gina looks like a Red Bull cautionary tale. I don't think she's slept for days. I don't think she could if she tried. But she confidently said that she and her tech team are just a

THE PITCH

few days from completing the app. It will copy everything on Brittany's phone by just sitting next to her with my phone on. I just have to hold on for a few more days.

More than an hour has passed, but I wait a little longer. If I'm passing a test, I want to be convincing. But I still have the same feeling I woke up with this morning—there's something wrong. I remind myself that Denise and Eva are operating drones somewhere in the blueness above me. Maxwell and his special agents are probably outnumbering the children in this park if they'd make themselves visible. And somewhere in the world, my father knows and is helping me. None of this protection, though, eases the sick feeling in my gut.

I exhale and stand. I need to keep to the schedule and it's time to go home.

Chapter Twenty-Five

When I came home from the park yesterday, there was no activity at the Halls'—no Brittany taking baby Kate for a walk in the evening, no collecting the mail, nothing. Guy came home at the usual time and left this morning on time.

I went to the park again this afternoon and sat on the bench in the sunshine for two hours. Brittany didn't come and Lot is nowhere to be seen. I drove straight to headquarters, where Audrey assured me again that their absence is a test. I need to stick to the routine and, if questioned, use a suspicious counterintelligence director as the excuse. But she also told me to follow my instincts. It all sounds operationally correct—stick to the routine is what I'd tell my officer if I was head of counterintelligence. But the voice in my head keeps telling me that something's wrong and I believe her.

Peace is something I haven't felt since I woke up yesterday morning. I need peace. I need to know what to do. Like the scripture in Isaiah, I'm promised peace if I am steadfast and trust in the Lord. If I remain in this space of not knowing, we won't accomplish our operation. Each hour that passes is more time for Brittany and the other SVR agents to go dark. I can't let that happen. To stop them from harming our country is my job.

I've prayed off and on for the last hour I'd be guided to do the right thing. No answer has come, but I know one will. I'm not hungry, but I eat dinner. It's too early to go to bed, but I'm so exhausted. I lay on the sofa and close my eyes for a minute to rest. The darkness is a welcome escape and my muscles relax. My shoulders flatten and my hips settle into the soft cushions.

The paper airplane sails through the air and lands on a branch in the cherry tree. Pink confetti blossoms shower Livvy's head and she trills out laughter. Seeing her delight as the petals fall around her head takes me to a place I haven't been in a long time. So filled with joy, I immediately send another paper plane into the pink blossoms. I want to stay here under the blooming "flower tree" of my youth with Livvy and all the paper airplanes I can get my hands on.

Wake up, Kate. It's time to go, says the voice in my head. I don't want to leave, so I grip a paper plane until I crush it. *You have to get up. Now.* The feel of the sofa under my hips and against my shoulders takes the place of blossoms and paper airplanes. The laughter is gone, replaced by the rhythmic tick of the clock on my wall. It tells me I've been asleep for a half hour, but I feel rested, as if I've slept for an entire night.

I sit up and remember what woke me. The fear has left and my instinct has taken over, filling me with a need to move forward. *Put the earrings on with the microphone and notify headquarters to record you*, says the voice. I get the earrings out of my purse and put them on, then text Gina, one star, our code to record me. She texts back with one star, telling me I'm good to go.

"I know this isn't planned, but I feel like I should go pay Brittany and Guy a visit to see if I can find out what's going on," I say out loud so headquarters records it and someone knows what I'm doing.

This seems like more than a friendly visit, though, and I stop in my entryway for a second. *Take your go bag.* I bring in a slow inhale and exhale, having my impression confirmed. Taking my go bag can only mean one thing—whatever I need to do will involve traveling. I turn in a slow circle, scanning the contents of my home to see what else I need. I get my purse from my bedroom and dump the contents, including the quick-change disguise Jake gave me, into my go bag. I always keep a quick change in my go bag, but two can't hurt. I'll want to use my real ID as much as possible to create a trail for headquarters to follow. But if I need to become someone else, I have the tools I need.

By habit, my gaze moves to the front of my refrigerator. As it has since I began dating John, it's covered with Livvy's drawings. One, in particular, catches my eye—the drawing of me on a plane. *You need to go.* I take the drawing off the fridge, fold it carefully, and put it in my go bag. I push aside the fear I associated with this drawing when Livvy gave it to me. There's no time for fear now.

The afternoon is just giving way to evening. There are a few shadows as I walk across the street and up Brittany's perfectly manicured walk. Without hesitation, I ring the doorbell. Heavy footsteps come toward the door and I know Guy will be answering it.

"Hey, Kate. Thanks for coming over. I was just going to text you and let you know we're ready," Guy says. He's harried but his usual happy self. Just inside the door are several pieces of luggage, including a car seat and a stroller. Adrenalin blooms across my face and down my neck. I grip the straps of my go bag until they cut into my fingers.

"Great," I say. I've been trained for moments like this—walking into the middle of something I'm supposed to be a part of but know nothing of.

"It's so nice of you to help Brittany on the flight to Florida. I can't go for another couple of days and her parents are dying to meet their granddaughter," Guys says. Brittany told me not long after we met that her retired parents live in Florida.

"Of course," I say. There's a good portion of information I'm supposed to know, so I can't ask too many questions. But I need to keep him talking. The more he tells me, the more headquarters knows, and the more information I have to figure out what's going on.

"Is that all you have?" he asks, motioning to my go bag on my shoulder.

"She won't need much," Brittany says, appearing next to her husband. She's holding a sleeping baby Kate, wrapped in the blanket I gave her. "It will be quick for Kate." My eyes lock onto Brittany's and bile bubbles up in the back of my throat. Like in the moment I knew she was Russian, I know now she's discovered I'm a double agent, and she's taking me to Russia.

Chapter Twenty-Six

There's only one Kate in front of the curtain in my mind, the Kate that must stay alive long enough to accomplish this operation.

"Let me hold her while you finish getting your things together," I say to Brittany. I step through the doorway and hold out my hands. Brittany's eyes narrow but she hands me baby Kate. The warmth of her limp body against my chest is so far from the world I'm in right now. Vulnerable emotions stumble through the curtain in my mind and land on their knees. I want to turn and run, but I can't and Brittany knows this—I'd be risking my life and the life of the baby. I have to work smart and I'm sure it's what she'd do, too. *Stay focused*, says the voice in my head. Emotions return to their place behind the curtain, but they crawl to get there.

Brittany and Guy walk into the kitchen, far enough away for me to do the one thing I *can* do. I lean my face next to baby Kate. Her light, feathery breath brushes my cheek. She smells of baby—milk, baby wipes, and the unique smell of her skin. I say a quick prayer for strength, then say what I need to say.

"Your little lips look like rosebuds." *Rosebud* is the code word John, the team, and I decided on to signal that I've been compromised. Headquarters just erupted as I stand in the quiet entryway of the Halls' home holding the child named after me.

Like me, everyone on my team is trying to figure out how I was made—what alerted Brittany that I'm a double agent. It could have been any number of things, but I can't give my mental energy to figuring it out now and neither can those at headquarters. I also can't start mentioning obvious details about where we're going. Brittany will know I'm wearing a wire and feeding information to someone. And once I'm in the air, the microphone on my earrings won't work anymore. I have to sound normal, move forward, and try to stay a step ahead of Brittany. This operation just turned into a race against time for Gina—I need the app and I need it now.

"Okay, everyone in the car or you ladies will miss your flight," Guy says. He picks up the car seat and two pieces of luggage and heads to the garage. The next few minutes are the normal confusion of loading the car. Brittany keeps giving me side looks when Guy is distracted, but I don't look back or respond. I'm sure she has many questions for me, but I can't waste my mental energy playing into the tension between us. She will take me to a place where I can be killed with as little attention as possible—a deserted alley in the slums of Moscow—and get back here to keep her cover with Guy. Once I get the text from Gina that the app is operational, it will be five seconds to copy Brittany's phone. I'll get a second text telling me the copy was successful, and then I run. I have burner phones, money, and disguises for two different profiles.

Teams will be sent to retrieve baby Kate and apprehend the people working with Brittany here in the US. The gathering of intel will begin before I ever make it back here. But if Brittany's on Russian soil when the app goes operational, we won't be able to arrest her—she'll have immunity. But she won't ever be able to return to America.

I keep working the case in my mind as we drive to the Dulles International Airport. I have to give Brittany credit. She keeps her cover believable—she and Guy exchange the normal banter a couple would have before such a trip. He's worried about sending his wife and baby on ahead and she's excited to see her parents but will miss Guy until he comes. It's all a very convincing show. But for Guy, it's his life, and he believes it all. My pretend job is to see Brittany and baby Kate safely to the waiting "parents" then turn around and catch a redeye home. Brittany's plan for me is quite different.

I play my part as Guy unloads the luggage at the airport—I'm the friend making traveling with an infant easier. My mind wants to go on a hundred different paths, but I force it in one direction—stay alive until my phone vibrates with the two texts from Gina. At some point Brittany will take my phone from me, but I have two burner phones, charged and on, sewn into the lining of my go bag. When I became a double agent, I gave Gina my go bag ID along with the numbers of the burner phones.

Brittany smiles and waves as Guy pulls away from the curb. As soon as he's out of sight, the smile drops from her face and she turns toward me. I raise my eyebrows in question. She's in charge here, not me.

"If you don't do exactly what I tell you, Olivia dies while John watches. You got it?" she says. My ears ring as nausea spins my head. I knew at some point she'd verbally threaten me and those close to me, but nothing prepares you for hearing the words. Brittany's eyes are unblinking and hard, her jaw clenched, but her hand that holds onto the stroller shakes.

"I don't know what you think you have on me, but it's not true," I say. "I've followed all the protocols. All the intel I've given you is clean." Every emotion inside me is behind the curtain. All Brittany sees is the calm confidence of an agent who is telling the truth. What I just said contained complete sentences. My eyes are normal and my breathing steady—all signs that I'm telling the truth. This will plant a seed of doubt about whatever she has on me, which could buy me some valuable time.

"Shut up and stay close to me," Brittany says. I fold my arms and nod, waiting for her to make a move, but she stands still, intently watching the cars come and go as passengers are dropped off. Gratefully, baby Kate has slept through all of this. I offer a quick prayer for her safety, reminding myself that Brittany has to keep her safe—the missing child of a Pentagon employee would cause unwanted attention for Russia.

After a few minutes, a gray SUV pulls up in front of us. Brittany opens the passenger rear door and puts baby Kate in a car seat that's already installed. A man is driving, and a woman is in the passenger seat. They both have on hats and sunglasses, and neither turn to look at us.

Without a second glance, Brittany shuts the door on her sleeping daughter. She puts all the luggage in the back of the SUV, closes the tailgate, and slaps the window twice. The SUV immediately pulls out and in seconds, is gone.

"Your parents from Florida?" I ask. Brittany glares as she walks past me. I keep in step with her as we enter the terminal. I assume baby Kate will be with the Russian couple I just saw. Guy believes this couple to be Brittany's parents who are enjoying their golden years in sunny Florida. When Brittany has taken care of me, she'll fly back to Florida and be waiting with her parents and daughter when Guy arrives. It's what I'd do.

I'm sure there's some type of accident planned that will be a believable cover for my death—a late-night car accident on my way home from the airport. Perhaps I'll be hit by someone head-on, our cars exploding on impact. At least it will look like that. A second body will be found with convincing ID—not the work of Lot, though. I'm certain Lot is in Moscow waiting for me. The Russians need me to disappear, and quickly.

A sign directs those taking international flights. Brittany shoots me a side glance as we turn and follow where the sign points.

Chapter Twenty-Seven

My phone is in the pocket of my jeans. I have on a short-sleeved white T-shirt and my hair down to cover the earrings—a typical outfit for a meet with Brittany, so she knows I'm not hiding anything in layers of clothing or a hair clip. I wish I wouldn't have followed this protocol, though. She's going to take my phone and go bag from me sometime and it can't be before the app goes operational—she'll most likely destroy my phones as soon as she finds them. If I could take one of the burner phones from the lining in my go bag without Brittany noticing, I could find somewhere to hide it on me. The phones are thin and narrow.

Brittany has our ticket information and boarding passes on her phone, and we make it through security without a hitch. It's a long walk to our gate—this is usually the case with international flights. With each step, I will my phone to buzz with a text, but it doesn't. Each shop and door we approach, I make a plan for escape. I'm sure Brittany knows I'm doing this, but she also assumes I'm not ready to announce to the intelligence community that

I'm a traitor—she believes I'm going to prove my loyalty to Russia even if it means getting on the plane. I offer another pleading prayer that my phone will buzz before we board.

When we arrive at the gate, my heart rate increases and sweat forms on my upper lip. Our flight—a nonstop to Moscow—boards in forty-five minutes. I discretely wipe off the sweat and take a few deep breaths through my nose. I was hoping for a little more time.

"I need to use the restroom," I tell Brittany. I really don't need to, but it's a chance for a moment without her watching me. She gives me an annoyed look but nods. She gets up and heads toward the women's restroom. I don't get to go by myself, which makes sense. But I still have my go bag and with a few private moments in a stall, I can hide a burner phone on me.

The bathroom is busy, but there are open stalls. Brittany leans against the wall by the door and motions with her head for me to go. It's a large bathroom and I pick the open stall the furthest from her line of sight. With distance and the constant flushing of toilets and running water as a noise mask, I can do what I need to do.

I sit on the edge of the toilet seat so my feet are in the correct position if Brittany walks down the aisle to checks. With a pencil, I rip the lining in my go bag and remove a burner phone. I make sure it's on, charged and muted. Then I rip the lining on the inside of the waistband of my jeans and slide the phone in. I've been wearing my T-shirt untucked, so the waist of my jeans is hidden. The only other place that wouldn't show would be my shoe and it's too risky—the phone could slide around and alter my walking. I rip open another section of the waistband lining and slide in a credit card and some cash. When Brittany takes my bag, I'll still be able to communicate and pay for public transportation.

As I double-check my phone, Livvy's drawing catches my eye. I don't have the time, but I take it out anyway and unfold it. I run my fingers across the lines of crayons and markers, missing her and John so much it takes my breath. What will I do if I actually have to get on the plane? Once in Russia, how will I escape from Brittany? What if Gina doesn't get the app done in time? Panic rises in me like water filling a tub.

You'll use your tradecraft and your instinct, says the voice in my head. *It will all work out.* These are familiar words that have been true in the past. I close my eyes and plead, once again, for guidance.

My eyes fly open and pinpricks of adrenalin move down my legs. Whether or not we realize it, we clearly define the small space of a bathroom stall as ours while we occupy it. Anyone or anything crossing these boundaries is a shocking invasion, like what I'm experiencing right now.

I move my left foot to get a better view of what is crossing the invisible barrier between my stall and the one on my left. I make out the scratchy sound of metal on tile, and watch as a can of Red Bull slowly slides across the boundary to my side. Two fingers push the can a few inches further, two fingers with red nail polish I'd recognize anywhere—Gina.

My body sways with uncontrolled relief and I quickly pick up the can. The two fingers with red nail polish remain and I lock my fingers around them. Connection to my world! My team is here, helping me. I'm not alone. *Your relationships will save you*, the voice in my head reminds me. *Drink the Red Bull and go.*

I give Gina's fingers a squeeze, then let go. The door to her stall opens and the sound of her leaving and another woman entering blends in with the rest of the background noise. I can tell by the shoes of the new occupant of the stall that it's not Brittany. Gina can get away, and I have a few more precious seconds.

There is a familiar square of duct tape on the side of the Red Bull can where Gina injected the drink with a tracking agent. It's the same tracking agent that saved me on our last operation, though I believe she has been working on it, so it lasts longer in my system and tracks an even further distance. On the side of the can, written in bright pink lipstick, is one word that causes my heart to leap—soon. My team is arming me with layers of protection, so if everything is taken from me, they'll be able to see where I am, even on the other side of the world.

I pop the opening of the can and gulp the liquid. The same chemical aftertaste is there as when I last drank the tracking agent. I rip open a protein bar and eat half of it in one bite, so the Red Bull doesn't hit my system on an empty stomach. I put the can in the small waste sack in the stall and flush the toilet. I count to five—the time it would take me to zip and button my pants—then walk out of the stall, knowing that I'm now a bright-pink dot on the screen of Gina's laptop.

Chapter Twenty-Eight

Moscow isn't a vacation destination, even in the summer months, so the flight is only half full. Brittany points me toward the window seat and she takes the aisle. Thankfully, I won't have to sit for nine and a half hours with my leg touching hers. Though we have an empty seat between us, I'll keep my go bag on the floor as far from Brittany as I can.

The Red Bull is doing its magic in my system and it's all I can do to keep my hands from shaking. I keep my arms folded and act as if I'm cold, though it's warm and muggy as the passengers file by and take their seats. I don't put my phone on airplane mode and neither does Brittany.

I have the duration of the flight to decide what I'll do in Moscow—how long will I wait for the app before I make a break and run? Will Brittany have a car waiting for us? Will there be someone driving it? I'll have little control over my surroundings if I get in a car with her and a stranger. *You'll know exactly what to do*, says the voice in my head.

Brittany fought sleep for the first hour of the flight, then finally gave in. I can't sleep even if I tried. Each hour drags by as I look out the plane window at the black sky. Panic keeps trying to find a crack it can seep through, but I fight it off with prayer. I repeat the Isaiah scripture over and over in my mind, feeling its message in my soul. I try to empty my mind of the jumble of scenarios and strategies, and simply trust—trust my training, my team, the love John and I share, and the Lord.

I want to do my job. I want to gather the intel I was tasked to gather—the names of those working with Brittany. She and Lot will end up on an international terrorist watch list and will be caught if they ever try to leave Russia, but we can find everyone else.

The plane tilts slightly downward and Brittany's eyes pop open. I give her my best "I wonder what Mother Russia would think if she knew you slept" look because I can. It's petty of me because we both know that spies eat when they can and sleep when they can. But her casualness is unnerving me. She has taken nothing from me, relaxes enough to sleep, and has said next to nothing. None of the normal protocols matter to Brittany now. I've become a loose end to tie up. I've been that before and it's not fun. This casualness points to what I know is waiting for me—at the first opportunity I'll be killed and Brittany will hop on a plane to Florida.

The captain announces our descent into the Vnukovo International Airport. After a long, dark night, the light of mid-morning fills the plane's cabin and lifts my heart. Lot will have to kill me in broad daylight, which I'm sure he can do, but it won't be ideal circumstances. This inconvenience may buy me some time.

When the wheels of the plane touch the runway, I close my eyes and pray to feel the subtle vibration of one of my phones. It could happen any minute. Gina can see me as I walk off the plane and into the airport terminal. I push the fear behind the curtain and allow my instinct to take center stage. Each step I take, I pull tactics forward in my mind while pushing others aside. I let my spy brain take over—the machine part of me.

Brittany looks groggy and annoyed as we wait in the customs line. The Vnukovo Airport is filled with metal and gray—a very Soviet look. The ceiling is made of hundreds of metal bars crisscrossing, creating a mass of triangles. If it weren't for the glass windows lining one wall, it would feel like a giant cage.

I listen to Brittany switch effortlessly from perfect English to Russian as she talks to the customs agent. When it's my turn, I brace myself to answer the questions he'll ask me, but he waves me through. I look at Brittany as she slowly smiles, then back at the customs officer. His face is blank—a practiced, emotionless stare, but I catch his jaw slightly twitch as he swallows. Perhaps I'm not the only one who knows my fate. I try to force the panic back, but there's no stopping the adrenalin from transitioning me into an enhanced, slow-motion perception of my surroundings. Adrenalin is a fantastic drug. Everything you see, hear, and feel is sharper as it magically courses through your system.

As we make our way through the busy terminal, I notice scuffs on a man's dress shoe. The black marks look like lightning bolts against the brown leather. A woman drops her wallet and swears, one of the crude words Brittany screamed when she was in labor. A child wheels a small pink suitcase past us. The wheels squeak in a rhythmic pattern that reminds me of a time I spent in a garbage bin escaping headquarters. The pink of the suitcase is bright and sparkles. Livvy would like it.

We walk through the entrance and out into a sunny midday in Moscow. Brittany remains silent, but I watch her every move . . . and she changes before my eyes.

In training, we were taught that when a person returns to the place of their birth—where they spent their childhood—that the very cells of their body remember. The connection between Brittany and her country happens right in front of me. To be in the place she came from and breathe the air changes her. To describe it would be futile other than to say she has come home. In training, they taught us that no disguise, no dialect, no years of living in a country can reproduce the authenticity I just witnessed, and now I believe it. No matter how convincing an American Brittany was, it only took a few steps on Russian soil for her to become who she really is—Russian.

We walk down a sidewalk toward a parking lot and I immediately gage the distance—two hundred yards. Should I run at the end of the sidewalk? My heart pounds against my chest, beating its way to freedom. *Hang on. Just a few more seconds*, says the voice in my head. What if I don't have a few more seconds? In a few more seconds, I won't have a way out. *You will. A path will be made for you.*

We walk past a line of cars and head toward a second when Brittany stops. Adrenalin fires through my body in a confusion of fear and relief as I experience two things at once—the sickening smell of Lot's cigarette smoke and the feel of all three phones vibrating at once.

Chapter Twenty-Nine

Count, says the voice in my head. I turn and face Brittany so my phone, waistband, and go bag are inches from the phone in her purse.

One-one-thousand, two-one-thousand, I count in my head.

"So, what was it?" I ask. I have five seconds to find out what blew my cover. The smell of Lot's cigarette intensifies, but I don't need to smell it to know he's close—I can feel his gaze on me.

Three-one-thousand.

Brittany looks me in the eye and I see her exhaustion. That's good. I know I can outrun a tired woman who just gave birth and a chain-smoking, old fat man.

"What a surprise to find out your daddy is still in play," Brittany says. A weight drops in my stomach, so heavily my knees almost buckle. So that was it. They found out my father is still a spy and not a horrible person I hate.

Four-one-thousand, five-one-thousand. All three phones vibrate at the same time that a tearing pain shoots across my scalp. My jaws and spine are on fire as my head jerks back. Lot holds my hair in his left fist. The bad ones always go for the hair first. My lungs fill with his rancid breath as he laughs.

In one satisfying motion, I drive my right foot into Lot's instep and my left elbow into his nose. He releases my hair as blood covers his mouth. Something falls out of his right hand and I see a syringe on the ground. That's how an assassin handles a kill in broad daylight.

Brittany throws a punch with her right fist but I duck and it lands on Lot's shoulder. He gurgles out some swear words through the blood. I give Brittany a hard kick in her right knee and she crumbles onto the pavement.

Run to your left, says the voice in my head. Gripping my go bag against my chest, I turn and launch myself forward. *Keep running through the cars.* I weave through a group of parked cars and come out the other side. The sound of running footsteps is behind me, a good distance back, though.

"Katie!" I look ahead, past the next group of cars, and see a tall man standing next to a dark car. His hair and beard are reddish brown and he wears dirty, worn work clothes. But no disguise could hide the set of his shoulders and strong stance.

"Dad," I whisper. I maneuver through the next group of cars in seconds. I want to throw myself into his arms, but as soon as I approach, he opens the back driver side door.

"In, Katie, and out the door on the other side. Pull the lever as you crawl by. Quickly. And stay down," he says. He gives me a smile that goes all the way to his eyes and it's better than any hug. I feel as if I could fly away from here.

"I love you," I say and crouch into the back of the car. A large box with a lever sits on the seat and I know instantly what my father has set up. I pull the lever and a waist-high version of myself inflates. It's a jack-in-the-box—known in intelligence as a JIB—and was a go-to device to avoid Russian surveillance during the Cold War. It's old-school but still very effective. My team and I used it on our first operation.

"You'll be safe now, Katie. Do what the woman says. Love you, too," my dad says. I maneuver past the JIB and crawl out the back passenger door. Across the way, a woman is standing next to an old-looking brown car. Crouching down, I run the few steps it takes to get to the car. The woman—the mother of the girl with the pink suitcase—opens the back driver's side door and I crawl inside. Her daughter, who looks about five years old, is watching something on her mom's phone. She glances at me and puts one finger up to her lips, telling me to be quiet. Then with the same finger, she swipes the phone screen and her eyes are back to the device. It's as if this little girl rescues spies with her mom every day.

"Down on the floor and pull that blanket over you," the woman says urgently. I do as she says but can still hear my dad drive away, followed by the sound of running footsteps and coughing. A wheezing Lot hollers from across the drive, asking the woman if she has seen a young lady with dark hair. The woman tells Lot that she saw someone who fits that description get in the car that just drove away. There's no sound of Brittany.

My heart is pounding in my chest and I desperately try to slow my breathing. I curl myself around my go bag and try to be small and silent. A car pulls up and I hear Lot scream a horrible name at Brittany, demanding to know what took her so long. A door slams and tires squeal, and then it's quiet. My father will lead Brittany and Lot on a chase and, hopefully, lose them on the streets of Moscow. Just like with John, my father has made a path for me where there was none, but at an enormous risk. Tears burn my eyes and I cover my mouth to stop the sob. The woman gets in the car and starts the engine.

"Are you okay? There's a bottle of water next to my daughter on the seat," the woman whispers. The woman speaks English well but with a heavy Russian accent. I muffle a *thank you*, reach up, and find the bottle. I turn my head to the side and gulp the cool water, smearing what I spill across my hot face. The blanket is scratchy and smells of exhaust. It probably has been in their trunk for a while.

"Thank you for everything," I whisper but with a clear voice. "You and my father are taking an enormous risk for me."

"Your father is a good friend. My husband and I would do anything to help his daughter. He knew if you saw him, you'd run to him. And for me, you should know more than anyone that I'm practically a ghost—a mom driving around with her child in the back seat. No one suspects me," she says.

I know the KGB never considered women a threat. Though the SVR will train women from birth to be sleeper cells in America, perhaps some of the old KGB attitude toward women has remained. Right now, I'm grateful it has with Lot. He didn't consider walking over to the woman's car to inspect it. I pull the blanket back a little, enough to see the little girl smile at me, then return to the phone and whatever is more interesting than the strange lady under the blanket on the floor of the car.

"So, my father has told you about me?" I ask. The woman chuckles and then tells me to hold on. I feel the car turn around and go back the way we came—toward the airport.

"Your father is proud of you and your team of mom spies. And he approves of your man, John." I smile at her, referring to John as my man. Perhaps that's how the Russians translate a boyfriend. The car comes to a gentle stop.

"When I tell you, open the door and get out. Stay low. As I hand my husband his lunch, you'll slide into an open compartment in the side of his truck. You'll have to lie down. He'll take you to the plane," she says.

I hear what sound like a diesel engine park beside us. I wish I could leave this family something as payment, perhaps the cash I have in my waistband. But using American currency in Moscow would definitely put them on some kind of radar. I offer a quick prayer on their behalf, that they'll be safe, like ghosts.

"Okay, now," the woman says. I slowly pull the door handle.

"Thank you, again," I whisper and crawl out. I look back at the little girl who glances at me, smiles again, then goes back to her phone.

Next to the car is a white utility truck. A large rectangular compartment is open. I don't get a clear look at her husband, but I hear their exchange in Russian—him thanking her for lunch and her reminding him not to be late for dinner. There's a rustle of paper as I lie down and pull the compartment door shut. There are vents and plenty of air, but it's tight. We drive for what feels like fifteen minutes, making several turns. I close my eyes to slow the motion sickness that's causing my head to spin and bile to rise in my throat.

When the truck finally stops, I exhale a long breath. The heavy roar of an airplane engine is the best sound in the world. The compartment door opens and fuel-filled air floods my face. The man has a kind face with brown eyes. He smiles and leans into my ear so I can hear him above the engines.

"Run. Your man waits for you on the plane."

Chapter Thirty

I take the stairs to the plane door three at a time. John is waiting for me just inside the door. I bury my face in his neck and let myself melt into his arms. He smells of faded cologne and travel.

"The baby?" I ask.

"We don't know. Maxwell sent a team to get her and apprehend the couple," John says.

"And Guy?"

"He's at headquarters. They're talking to him." A door opens behind us and the pilot sticks his head out.

"We gotta leave. Now," he says. The plane is a private jet sent by Neal. It's the same one we've used in past operations, usually to rescue me from a dangerous situation. It's beautiful, with a leather interior and John and I have it to ourselves. This is a kindness from Neal I appreciate because I have many questions for John. But right now, we need to get out of Russia. John and I take our seats facing each other and the plane is in the air in a matter of minutes.

"Have you heard from my father?" I ask.

"He's safe. Don't worry about your dad. He knows what he's doing," John says.

"He saved me. All of you did. It would have been rough getting away from Brittany and Lot. But it will put my dad on the Russians' radar. He doesn't need more of that," I say.

"He'll disappear as soon as this is over. But so far, Brittany still has no idea her phone has been copied. She's still trying to find your dad, which gives us time. And I'm sure Lot has disappeared," he says.

"What intel do we have so far?" I ask. John exhales through his nose and closes his eyes for a second.

"Brittany is one of eight women. Maxwell will apprehend all seven at once so there's no time for warnings to be sent between the women. This was quite the operation Putin masterminded. These women are married to men in the DOJ, NSA, the White House staff, and there were two other men at the Pentagon. It's ugly," John says. My ears are ringing and not because we're rapidly gaining altitude.

The captain comes on the intercom and tells us we can undo our seat belts and move around. I click mine off and move across to sit by John. He pulls me close as I curl up next to him.

"This was huge. I can't imagine the damage they've done, and not just to our country. There are families that are torn apart," I say. John nods and lays his cheek against my hair. His throat moves as he swallows.

"All but one of these women have children. The children are young, though. Who knows what they'll remember," John says.

"This has got to feel like you're reliving Clare all over again," I say.

"In a way, it does. But I've come a long way since then. I can be some support to these men, especially Guy," he says.

"I'll be there for little Kate, just like I'll be there for Livvy. They'll have questions when they get older and I want to be one of the people who answers them," I say. John smiles and then leans over and kisses me.

"It will be hard for Guy to imagine it now, but there's hope for him to have a family again, to have a partnership with a woman he can trust and who will love his child like her own," he says. Tears fill my eyes and I don't hide them. I lean up and kiss John back, then rest my forehead against his.

"Thank you," I whisper. "Thank you for being here on this plane with me." I smile and pull back so I can see his face. "The couple that smuggled me back to the airport referred to you as my man. The woman said that my father approves of my man and her husband said my man was waiting for me on the plane," I say. This brought a smile to John's face.

"So, from now on, I want you to call me your man," he says. My chuckle turns into a jaw-stretching yawn.

"My man. Okay. You got it," I say around the yawn. It's been over twenty-four hours since I've slept and the effects are getting to me. Though Gina's tracking agent is still in my system and will be for days, the Red Bull is long gone.

"How about you curl up here next to your man and sleep for a while? I'll wake you up if I hear any updates," John says. I rest my head on his shoulder and sleep pulls me under in minutes.

Throughout the rest of the flight, we learn Maxwell orchestrated seven teams of FBI special agents who apprehended the seven women, all of whom proved to be just like Brittany—Russian spies stealing classified intel from their husbands.

Baby Kate is in the safe custody of the FBI and on her way back to her father. The couple posing as Brittany's parents were apprehended. They are a part of an extensive support network aiding the eight female spies with their covers, mostly acting as extended family and friends. From what we've heard so far, a good portion of this support group has been caught. But some were able to get away and go dark. They'll be on watch lists if they try to leave the country.

Through a cryptic text to John, we learned my father is safe and enjoyed leading Brittany on a lengthy chase in and around Moscow until she was taken into custody by the Russian police. She will most likely be turned over to the SVR and "punished" for compromising her cover. This was such a huge undertaking on Putin's part, I don't think Brittany will live to see next week. After the torture she'll endure, death will be a welcome relief. The seven other women will beg to spend their lives in an American prison. If they're shipped back to Russia, they could suffer the same fate as Brittany.

I'm groggy but rested by the time we land in DC. That's a good thing, because John and I will go directly to Langley for a debriefing. We'll also have a chance to see Guy and baby Kate.

Chapter Thirty-One

It's midnight by the time John and I walk into headquarters. It's so busy, though, it appears as if it's midday. There will be months of debriefings and damage control from this operation and it begins immediately.

I walk across the gray CIA emblem on the floor of the entryway and it doesn't seem so gray as the day I found out who Brittany really was. Intelligence has had a huge win with the discovery of this Russian sleeper cell. But like most of our wins, there are lives destroyed in the process. The unearthing of lies is a gritty, painful process, and it always comes at the cost of betrayal. Truth is sacred and the innocent pay when we disgrace it. Today, Guy and other families will pay. Someday, baby Kate will pay, but I will be there to lessen the price for her. Neal greets us at the door of the conference room and enfolds me in a fatherly hug.

"You're safe and that's all that matters," he says. "Nadine and I are so relieved." I move from his arms into the arms of my team. They surround me, then pass me from one to the other. It's like coming home.

"You're here. You're safe," says Denise.

"I am," I say and give her another hug. She looks like a faded, exhausted version of her beautiful self. Eva is bouncing on her toes when she grabs hold of me.

"You did it. I'm so proud of you," she says. There's the slightest bit of fatigue around her eyes, but she could probably go another twenty-four hours at peak performance—training that came from years as a Border Patrol Agent. Despite the long hours, she still smells of fresh laundry, like my mother did.

"Oh, I can't stand it. Y'all get in these arms," Gina says and pulls me into a messy makeup hug—black mascara is striping her cheeks. Her hair looks like a two-day matted mass of blond curls and there are yellow stains the same color as Red Bull on the front of her white blouse.

"Thank you. You saved me," I say into her hair. She pulls away and wipes her face with a tissue Denise hands her.

"I was so afraid I wasn't gonna get that app done in time. My land, I thought I was gonna have a heart attack," she says.

"Maybe that was the case of Red Bull you downed," Denise says. Gina waves this off with her makeup-spotted tissue.

"Well, the Red Bull saved me again," I say. "I was so relieved to see that can come sliding under my bathroom stall." This brings a few chuckles. "Knowing I was a pink dot on your computer screen gave me the courage to get on the plane," I add. "I knew it was you. I'd recognize your red nail polish anywhere."

"I'll spare y'all the details, but it helped to have my laptop within close range of your phone, so Jake put me in some old lady get-up and I brought ya the Red Bull myself,"

Gina says. "There I was, lookin' like an old grandma sliding under bathroom stalls. No one noticed me, though. Everyone's lookin' at their phones." People were laughing at her description, but my eyes burned and I pulled her into another hug.

"Thank you for doing that," I say. These women would do anything for me and I love them. A frazzled Audrey came in and immediately gave me a hug.

"Great work. I know for certain your father is safe," she says. I exhale and thank her. "The baby will be here in a few hours, but let's get going." We take our seats around the conference table and begin the debrief.

At three in the morning, a light tap sounds at the door and a secretary tells us that baby Kate is here. Guy has been in a debrief at the Pentagon but is heading here to get his daughter.

"I'd like to see her," I say. Everyone nods as I stand and head to the door.

"She's down the hall, fourth room on the right. Agent Maxwell brought her and is with her now," the secretary says. I raised my eyebrows, and she smiled at my surprised expression. "I'll let you see for yourself," she says and heads down the hall in the opposite direction.

I walk toward the fourth door but stop before I reach it. There's a mix of humming and words. I take a few more steps and then I'm certain of what I'm hearing—singing. Can it be?

Two more steps give me a visual through the doorway. Maxwell is holding baby Kate, who's swaddled in a gauzy peach-colored blanket. She's awake and her eyes are locked on Maxwell's face.

You are my sunshine
My only sunshine
You make me happy when skies are gray

Maxwell has a remarkably pleasant voice, but what has me planted in the hallway and stunned into silence is the tenderness on his face. He's transformed. The smile reaches his eyes, but it's something more. I've seen a similar look recently and my mind flips through the past hours until it lands on the smile my father gave me before I got in the car. Maxwell has the look of a father on his face. I know he has three daughters and has been happily married for over thirty years. I've just never seen this side of him. Quick footsteps come up the hall toward me and a man brushes past and into the room.

"Is she here? Do you have her?" says Guy through a gruff sob.

"She's safe. She's right here," Maxwell says and hands Guy his daughter. Guy takes the baby and buries his face in his daughter's little chest. Silent sobs wrack Guy's body and he falls to his knees, rocking back and forth. Maxwell leans down and puts his big hand on Guy's shoulder.

"She's whole and safe. We'll help you through this, son," Maxwell says, and gives Guy's shoulder a squeeze. Maxwell turns and comes out the door, shutting it behind him. When he sees me, I brace myself for his anger at having witnessed this vulnerable moment. But he comes over to me, the same tender expression on his face. "And you're whole and safe," he says to me, nods once, and then walks past me down the hallway.

Maxwell just keeps surprising me. There's so much I don't know about him, especially about him and my father's friendship. But what I know now is that Rolland Maxwell is capable of great tenderness and compassion, much like my father.

I push a button next to the door and a light comes on, showing that the room is occupied and shouldn't be disturbed. No one else should see Guy's grief. This time is just for him and his daughter.

Chapter Thirty-Two

There were no eyes following me on the way home, just the occasional side glance from the officer assigned to drive me. John needed to stay at headquarters. The officer and I didn't exchange words, just a *thank you* and *you're welcome* when he dropped me off. What happened with Brittany is an ongoing investigation, so I'm not at liberty to talk about it to anyone outside of my team. And really, what else is there to say? "So, how was Moscow?" The silent drive was nice, though, especially since it didn't involve Lot.

Walking into my home as Kate, the CIA officer—not the double agent—is even nicer. I stand in my entryway and scan the kitchen, living room, and down the hallway. All is as I left it, but there is a settled realness that draws a long exhale from my lungs. I no longer have to hide anything, at least not any more than I normally do.

I pick up my purse from the floor where I left it almost two days ago and methodically fill it with its contents from my go bag. I leave the extra quick-change disguise in my go bag and go to set it on the floor when I see Livvy's drawing. I carefully take the drawing out and set the go bag under my glass table for the next time I need it. And then I say a fervent prayer that it won't be soon.

There's a square of white exposed on the front of my refrigerator where the plane drawing I hold belongs, where I took it before I flew to Moscow. Someday, I'll explain to Livvy just how prophetic her drawing was, and the comfort it brought me. These lines of color on this white paper were a lifeline to me, a reminder of what's real as I made my way to Moscow and back. I place the drawing back where it belongs with two magnets and then run my fingers across it one more time.

Processing an operation once it is over is much like cleaning a house—you dispose of items that are no longer useful and put away those that are. I have found that it's important to have a place for everything. It can take a great deal of emotional energy to house emotions that have no place to call their own.

As I stand in front of Livvy's drawings, I close my eyes and slowly lift the curtain in my mind. This is much easier than what a block wall would involve. The emotions I kept hidden are waiting for me, easily accessed, just like Audrey said. I place each one where they belong. Some have new places and some fit comfortably back to where they've always been. Some are bruised and even bleeding, and I begin the slow process of healing them. This will take some time and patience. But I know how to do it—I've done it many times. The first step is always the same.

I open my eyes and take a deep breath. Healing can mean many things to many people, but I've found that there's one thing we all need to begin the process—comfort. I open the freezer, take out a pint of rocky road ice cream, and commit to it by ripping the lid off and throwing it away. It's a full-pint night.

Chapter Thirty-Three

John and I beat the dinner crowd at Manny's by an hour—the restaurant is empty. Within seconds of the bell jingling on the door, I am encircled by Manny's giant arms, the smell of oregano, bread dough, and sweat filling my lungs.

"You're safe. You're home and safe," Manny says. He lets me go and gives the same welcome to John. "Take your booth," he says and glides back to the kitchen. He called me earlier and told me I needed to come to dinner, so I hope that means he's heard from my father. John and I laugh as we brush flour off the front of our clothing and then sit at our booth. Manny is there in seconds.

"This is good advice. I think you should take it. And you too, young man," Manny says. His face is red, and it's not from cooking. He sets a Manny's Restaurant ticket on the table and thumps it twice with his sausage-size finger. "Water and bread," he says and skates back in the kitchen.

I turn the ticket over and on the back is a series of dots and lines—Morse code from my father. It just takes me a few seconds to transcribe it.

"Nice work, Katie. The Russians don't play nice. Perhaps think twice before you tangle with them again. Love you." I chuckle and hand the note to John to read. He smiles and then gives it back to me.

"Don't worry about your dad. He can take care of himself. Brittany and Lot were probably a pleasant diversion for him," John says. "I miss working with him." I turn my head to the side and smile.

"You do?" I ask. He nods and smiles.

"I've often wondered if I'll ever have the chance to work with him. I envy you those memories," I say. I know it's an impossible wish as long as my father has who he does after him.

"Perhaps we'll both have the chance to work with the great James McLean someday," John says. The thought makes my heart lift with hope. He would have to be free to do that, which is one of my greatest desires. Manny silently appears at our table with a tray filled with three loaves of bread and glasses of water.

"You're too thin. Both of you," Manny says and puts the bread and drinks on the table. "Tonight, I'm going to feed you like you should be fed and you're going to eat." Manny was worried about me, and I know he shows his love and concern for people by force-feeding them. It's not the first time John and I have experienced one of Manny's "love and concern" meals but something tells me this one will be especially large. I grab his hand before he leaves to go back to the kitchen.

"Manny, I'm sorry I worried you. But I'm so grateful you could send word to my father. You both saved me. Thank you, Manny, so much." Manny's face softens a bit and his heavy cheeks raise with his smile.

"It was nice to help your dad again, but not so nice when I know you're in danger. Like your father said, maybe think twice about it before you take on Russia again, okay?"

"I promise," I answer with my best smile. "And all this flying, I feel like I haven't eaten in days. I'm absolutely starving," I say. This is music to Manny's ears, and his large face lights up.

"I'll be right out. And it's on the house tonight," he says as he glides back to the kitchen.

"You know we're going to have to stuff ourselves to be back in his good graces again," I say to John after Manny's out of earshot.

"Well, you got us off to a good start," he says and tears a piece of bread for each of us.

"So, how'd it go with Guy today?" I ask. John met with him this afternoon for a personal visit, which Guy was grateful for—anything but another debriefing at the Pentagon. So far, there have been no charges brought against him. He told the Pentagon and the CIA that he never breached his security clearance—he never brought home classified information and never spoke to Brittany about anything he shouldn't have. I believe him. But it will take a long time to clear him, and he'll need family and good friends to support him as he goes through the process. His parents are coming out from Montana to stay and help him with baby Kate.

"He's still in shock. Betrayal on that level will take some time to get past. I told him about Clare and I think it helped that someone understands what he's going through."

"I'm glad you did that," I say. It almost destroyed John to learn his wife had been radicalized by jihadists before they were married. Though John had been trained to see deception, he never saw it in Clare. After he learned who she really was, he realized he'd ignored signs. As spies, we're trained to always look for what's wrong. He wasn't looking for signs that his wife was a terrorist, though, so why would he see them? I'm sure Guy would have never suspected that his wife was a Russian spy and his house full of bugs with Russian SVR agents listening to everything.

"I assured Guy he was a good father. That he saved little Kate. That's what's important." I nod and swallow my third bite of bread. We have to have one of these loaves gone by the time Manny brings our food.

"Neal told me something that day I discovered Brittany. He said that good fathers save their daughters. You and Guy saved your little girls just like my father saved me. A good father is many things, but he's always a guardian," I say. John's eyes shimmer in the dimming light from the window.

"Slide the bread over," Manny says. He has again silently appeared and holds a large tray heaped with platters of spaghetti, lasagna, ravioli, and a large bowl filled with some kind of soup. We push the bread aside as Manny fills our table with enough food for two large families. Rose won't have to cook for a week with what we'll end up taking home.

"This all looks so good," I tell Manny. He bobs his head once.

"Eat," he says but with a smile, and doesn't thump the table as hard as he did last time. He turns and slides past two tables to greet a family who just came in.

"I think we're making headway," I say. John laughs and then takes a large bite of lasagna. Like so many times before, I long to have my father with me. I hope wherever he is, he, like us, is celebrating a successful operation. Perhaps, someday, it will be with me.

I hope you enjoyed *The Pitch*. Thank you for reading it to the end.

There's more to come for Kate, John, and the team. I'm busy writing **Book 5**, so please go to my website, www.goawayimreading.com **here** to find out when it will be published.

Would you consider leaving a review for *The Pitch*? I'll try to make this as painless as possible. Click on the link below and you should be exactly where you need to be.
http://www.amazon.com/review/create-review?&asin=B0CBD2J573

If you're reading this in a paperback, there may be a wee bit of pain because you'll have to type the above link into a web browser, but you will have my eternal gratitude.

Thank you!

Also By Amy Martinsen

An Untapped Source Series
The Perfect Spy
Hold Your Breath
Loose Ends
The Pitch
The Secret Obituary Writer Series
The Secret Obituary Writer Book One
The Secret Obituary Writer Book Two
Hidden Springs Series
The Advice Columnist of Long Shot Lane

About Author

One of Amy's earliest memories is hiding between bales of hay to read *just one more chapter* instead of doing her chores. When her mother discovered this hiding place, Amy learned to climb trees and became very good at balancing on a branch while holding a book. She also developed extremely strong leg muscles. Amy still hides to read, but in much less dangerous places, like her closet and the laundry room . . . though she longs for the leg muscles of her youth. She also makes it her goal to write stories so engaging people will hide to read them. Perhaps even in a tree.

Visit www.goawayimreading.com to sign up for Amy's newsletter and find out what she's writing next.

You can also follow Amy on Facebook, Instagram, Amazon, BookBub, and Goodreads.

Made in the USA
Monee, IL
17 August 2023

41171215R00114